BUILDING FAMILY

COLLECTIONS

MEYARI MCFARLAND

CONTENTS

SPECIAL OFFER

The rainbow has infinite shades, just as this collection covers the spectrum of fictional possibilities.

From contemporary romances like *The Shores of Twilight Bay* to dark fantasy like *A Lone Red Tree* and out to SF futures in *Child of Spring*, *Iridescent* covers the gamut of time, space and genre.

Meyari McFarland shows her mastery in this first omnibus collection of her short fiction. Twenty-five amazing stories, all with queer characters going on adventures, solving mysteries, and falling in love are here in the first Rainbow Collection.

And now you can get this massive collection of short queer fiction, all of it with the happy endings you love, *for free!*

Sign up here for your free copy of Iridescent now!

You can find these and many other books at www.MDR-Publishing.com. We are a small independent publisher focusing on LGBT content. Please sign up for our mailing list to get regular updates on the latest preorders and new releases and a free ebook!

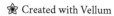 Created with Vellum

This collection is dedicated to my husband.

AUTHOR'S NOTE: SENSORY HOARD

I love dragons. Stories with dragons are some of my favorite things. The Unification series is full of dragons, all of whom have hoards. There's hoards of teapots, collected because of PTSD imprinting them on one dragon's mind. There's hoards of books, because, well, I'm a bit of a bookworm and I had to have a dragon hoard of books. That's just logical.

And then there's Mayami who has no hoard.

Who needs no hoard.

Hoards are stupid.

Friends, now. Friends are awesome, especially musical friends.

SENSORY HOARD

$\mathcal{M}$ ayami snorted, twin jets of fire shooting from her nostrils, head aching from the way her frill kept snapping upright and vibrating. Given that she'd gone up on the roof to perch and glare at everyone in her family, she didn't scorch anything. Didn't even singe the roof tiles, much as she'd like to. Her whole damn family was a giant pain in her tail. Figure out her hoard this, worthwhile way to spend her time that.

Like anyone's hoards were actually all that valuable. Old Youneda collected teapots of all things. Sure, they were occasionally worth something but mostly he just lay around drinking tea and sunning his fat belly. Stupid Ami claiming that Mayami was doomed to be a nobody doing nothing because she didn't have a 'proper' hoard yet.

Like Ami's hoard of silver spoons was worth bothering with. Easily packed, maybe, which was a darn good thing. Sooner she packed them all up and left home the happier Mayami would be. Of course, Kanoko would just start crying the instant Ami talked about her scholarship for college which set off Rio and then Natsuko would be yelling at all of them but especially Mayami.

"You're in a terrible mood."

Mayami turned and glowered at her best friend Shinji, hovering on his spelled float-board at its very highest level. Put his head three inches below the tip of her tail. He grinned at her. Then raised both eyebrows and sighed before looking into the backyard where Mayami's clutchmates were chattering together as they built a stack of logs for a bonfire.

"They're nagging about the hoard thing again, aren't they?" Shinji said in a flat enough tone that it wasn't a question.

"When don't they?" Mayami replied. "Come on. Let's go."

She flung herself off the roof, not towards the backyard but towards the front yard and the street. Their little cul-de-sac was quiet enough that she could get away with it. In busier parts of town, she'd smack right into a truck before she got a good glide going. Not here. The only trucks that came through were old Felix's battered pickup truck and delivery trucks hauling in books for Fuwa.

Now there was a really stupid idea for a hoard. There was only so much room for books and Fuwa couldn't seem to stop buying more and more. She'd seen his house. It was a miracle that he had room to turn around in there. Mayami'd bet anything that he had to sleep on top of his books and that just wasn't any good for keeping them in shape.

Mayami snorted jets of flame as Shinji flew after her on his float-board. She grinned to hear her clutchmates shouting at her for leaving and then flew three times faster when her mother shouted at her to fly her tail right back to the house and spend time with her siblings.

As if.

They were being rude. Mayami didn't have to deal with

3

that, no matter what everyone else said. She flicked her wings and went higher, up far enough that she was above the streetlights. Underneath her, Shinji skimmed along the street, dodging trash cans put out for collection and recycling bins. That was what she should hoard. Stupid things like stuff taken from recycling bins. It'd piss everyone off and then she could collect the memories of how disgusted everyone was.

Except no, that was gross. Why would she want someone else's trash? Yuck.

Why was it such a big deal what she collected anyway? If she had a hoard she couldn't go flying with Shinji all the time. She'd be stuck working and buying things or at least making them. Boring, boring, boring!

Shinji signaled Mayami before peeling off and heading up an alley between the old 7-11 that'd been converted into an apothecary and the little woodworking shop the dryads up in the wilds had set up with the help of the elves. Another turn had them racing each other up the street towards the bay and yeah, that was the ticket.

The wind went from questionably damp, rain looming, to crisp and swift-flowing with the scent of salt and dying sea critters. Oyster, mussel, slow-drying seaweed; a good smell, really, and one that always calmed her down.

Odd that it did. Fire-breathing dragons usually weren't happy around the ocean, but it made Mayami hum happily as they reached the bay and turned right, heading up around the point towards the park that used to be a golf course. The Opening hadn't been kind to the golf course. Smooth lawns had merged with swamps and bits of rocky promontory, creating a place that was fascinating to explore and completely forbidden for young kids.

Good thing Mayami, Shinji and their friends were all nearly grown up.

She heard the others long before she saw them, tucked

away inside a grove of cedar and lilac bushes. Ratnam had his drum. The throb of the thing fluttered the membranes of her wings, vibrated the firebox in her throat. From Shinji's grin, he heard Ratnam, too. After that it was the sound of Kanti and Gyeong's flutes, high and shrill, mixing with Sascha's little ukulele.

"Good call," Mayami called down to Shinji as she came in for a landing and then ran next to his side instead of flying. Trees were too high around here for flying anyway.

"Looked like you could do with some jam time," Shinji said.

His grin finally eased Mayami's frill back down from full alert. Which was good. If she'd kept it up much longer she'd've had a headache that made her snap everyone's heads off and they really didn't deserve it. Ratnam looked up when Mayami poked her head through the lilacs, grinning his sharp-toothed grin at her.

The tiny coral snakes decorating his head ignored her, bobbing in time with the music the way Ratnam didn't. Yet. He would soon enough. Ratnam head-banging was an awe-inspiring sight. Add in the way he danced, and it was enough to make Mayami's tail and wings start twitching to dance herself.

"Hey Mayami," Ratnam said. He kept on drumming, just moved to a softer, quieter beat. "Wondered if you'd show up."

"Anything to get away from my family," Mayami said.

She used a wing to push the lilacs and cedar branches aside for Shinji and then slithered through them once he was in the clearing. Shinji nodded to Ratnam before going and sitting next to Sascha who didn't smile, didn't even move at all. Her eyes were milk-white today, matching with the full moon that would rise this evening. Hair had gone white-blond, too, so it must be about time for a super-tide.

Sasha's fingers went still on the ukulele. One hand

reached out to brush over Shinji's wrist and wasn't that good to see? Neither of them was about to admit they were sweet on each other but Mayami could see it. Smell it. Sascha knew. With her nose, she had to. A mix of were and fey blood meant that she didn't act like a human but Mayami knew that she loved like one.

Good for Shinji there. If she were a little more fey Mayami wouldn't ever let Sascha touch.

"They're being brats again?" Kanti asked.

She and Geyong were identical twins, except that Geyong identified as male and Kanti as female. Purely choice on their parts. They were dryad-blood and had no distinct physical gender to mess up how people looked at them.

"Yep," Mayami said. She curled around the edge of the clearing, her tail twitching behind Sascha and Shinji, her head behind Ratnam. One wing went up to make an awning over Kanti and Geyong. "What are you going to hoard? When are you going to get serious and collect something? Why can't you just settle down and be a proper dragon like your siblings? I get so sick of it."

"But you're still young," Sascha said in her whispery voice. No frown but the way her fingers caressed the belly of her ukulele showed her concern. "It's too soon for you to settle on a hoard."

"I know that, and you know that," Mayami said with a gusty sigh, this time without any flame so that she didn't hurt her friends, "but my clutchmates are all soooo sure that they know exactly what they'll hoard so of course I have to do the same thing as them. I mean, Kanoko was talking about how she already knew exactly what house she wanted down the street."

"Is she trying to convince your parents to buy it for her?" Shinji asked.

He rolled his eyes when Mayami growled. Both Kanti and

Gyeong shook their heads while Sascha tutted her tongue. She started playing, fast and hard, which made Shinji pull out his harmonica and then Ratnam was drumming like he wanted to call down the moon.

Kanti and Gyeong grinned before lifting their flutes and playing like they were trying to pull souls out of the trees to dance with them all.

A moment later the dryad of the grove manifested to dance in the middle of the clearing. Mayami laughed and stood so that she could dance with the dryad, bowing and shifting through its green long limbs and smiling at its indistinct face. She kept her wings tight but drummed the earth in the center of the clearing with her feet, thumping her tail against her belly in time with the deepest of Ratnam's beats.

All the worries about her family faded away as the music swirled around her. Every dance step drove Mayami's anger outwards and then away, leaving peace and contentment. The dryad made the trees dance with them, cedars bowing and shifting as if there was a huge storm coming in. The lilac pollen billowed and swirled around her head. It coated her face, her wings, her neck, but didn't fall down to make it hard for the others to breathe.

Took until Mayami was starting to huff and pant streams of steam for Ratnam, Shinji, Kanti and Gyeong to slow to something more gentle. Sascha kept on playing but it changed from the hard-fast-rage-defiance to hard-fast-joy of a fey who was having enough fun to summon the Old Magic back to the world.

Mayami hummed and moved to rest her nose against Sascha's knees at the same time that Shinji set down his harmonica so that he could gently shake Sascha's shoulder.

"Hey," Mayami said. "Still here?"

She let her breath go steamy over Sascha's fingers even though that meant putting heat onto her ukulele. Normally

7

it'd get Mayami's nose swatted but this time Sascha's fingers slowed. Then she blinked, the white of her eyes going green and clear. Sascha looked at Mayami, really looked at her, and then laughed.

"You've already started your hoard," Sascha said, grinning as her eyes slowly drifted back to white, like fog drifting over a cedar valley until it blocked the trees.

Mayami reared back, shaking her head. "No, I haven't."

"You have," Sascha said. Her grin stayed wide and engaged even as she lost her sight of the physical world again. "You just need to figure it out."

"Huh." Ratnam grunted. When Mayami looked his way, he was grinning, and all his coral snakes were looking straight at her. "I think you're right, Sascha. Cool. I can handle that."

Then it was Kanti and Gyeong laughing and playing a little jig on their flutes while the dryad melted back into its trees. Mayami huffed at them. What hoard? She didn't collect anything. All she wanted was to play music and sing and dance with her friends. Keeping a stupid hoard didn't make sense. It'd just tie her down instead of letting her go where the music took her.

"Mayami," Shinji said after Mayami started huffing and sending sparks up into the air despite her best intentions, "it's us. It's the music. It's dancing. You're hoarding the whole... experience of being part of a band and playing. You're the one who brought us together. You made sure we all had the instruments we wanted. You arrange for us to go places and play. I mean, come on. That whole thing at the Fair last month? That was you. We'd never have gone if it weren't for you setting it up."

Mayami opened her mouth to disagree but.

But.

That, huh. That made sense. A lot of sense. Not that she could convince her parents that it was a worthwhile thing because no way would they accept a hoard that was memories and experiences instead of something solid. Something valuable that people would...

...pay money for.

"Um."

Ratnam grinned at Mayami as she flopped belly first into the center of the clearing. "You got an idea?"

"The High Elves always want new things," Mayami said. She waved one wing over her shoulders as she tried to work the idea out. "So do the fey. And there are mages who can pull a memory out of your head and make it visible for other people. Add some pixie dust to that and you could get other people to feel what you felt."

"...That could work," Sascha said. She blinked about a thousand times, really fast. "I'd pay for that, honestly. Not for music, mind you, but most of my fey relatives would love to experience some of our music. Any mortal music, for that matter. They don't have music like we do."

"The dryads would enjoy it, too," Gyeong said. "Most of them don't leave their groves so they're limited on experiences. You could travel to groves, share the memories of music, maybe experience their music, too. It's really different from what we do."

"A music hoard," Mayami said slowly. Her tail started quivering, nearly wagging even though there really wasn't room for that here inside the grove. "That. I could do that. I'd love that. Going all over the world listening to music and then sharing it? That would be... I could do that my entire life and never get tired of it."

She jumped back up to her feet, wings quivering with the need to go find out if it would even work. There was that mage in the cul-de-sac, the new mixed blood one who was so orange-skinned. He wasn't very strong, but he knew a lot. Mayami would just best that he could point her towards the right spells to use. And Felix knew all about pixie dust. He smoked that stuff constantly. If anyone could tell her how to ask the pixies for dust that let you experience the joys of another person, Felix would be the one. And then the wolf pack out on the other end of town had a really big, really healthy pixie nest.

It could work.

She could hoard music. Music and dancing and the joy that came from sharing it with people you loved. Mayami laughed as Ratnam waved for her to head out. Shinji grinned and waved, too, staying by Sascha's side. The twins, heck, they'd stay all night in the clearing if they could.

Mayami slithered through the cedars and lilacs and then launched herself up into the air. Mom and Dad would have so many questions but that was okay. It was a plan. An idea. Something that finally, finally, finally made Mayami excited instead of furious. Let her siblings get all wrapped up around stupid little trinkets. Her hoard was going to be the very best hoard possible. It wouldn't take up any space and she'd get to do so many things while collecting it.

Ami was going to look like she'd bit into a lemon!

She laughed and blew a jet of fire for the pure joy of it. The wind blew it back in her face, swirling it over her ears, her horns and frill and then down her spine like tiny whirlpools of flame. Mayami started singing as she flew. Her hoard.

Mayami laughed as she did a barrel roll. Her perfect, impossible hoard.

AUTHOR'S NOTE: FAMILY IN PROGRESS

*S*omeday, in the future long after I'm dead (sadly), I expect that humanity will have space stations all through the solar system. I also expect that someday, even longer after I'm dead, humanity will set out to other solar systems in some kind of ship. Personally, I expect us to start with generation ships. It'll be a whole pioneer movement, just spreading out in a cloud from Earth instead of across the American plains.

Humans will still be humans, though. That's the thing. Humanity had done some incredible stuff over the eons. Horrible stuff, too. There are good humans and bad humans and we're all mixed up, doing our best (or worst).

What gives me hope for those long-in-the-future descendants is that they'll find ways to make their own homes. Their own families. Might not look anything like what we have in the here and now, but it'll happen.

And that's beautiful.

1. SUSHILA VLAHOVIC

*C*hi leaned back against the door to xyr quarters, slowly sliding down to the floor. What a day. What an incredible, horrible, amazing, wonderful day. Xe still couldn't believe that they had passed out of Old Earth's solar system. How could that be possible? They'd been traveling since the day after Chi left school, three solid years. And now they'd left Old Earth's influence, gone outside of not just it's sunlight but also the solar well and even the Oort Cloud.

They were free.

Chi was free.

That'd been amazing, watching everything happening on the monitors, listening on xyr pad as xe worked. The entire foundry floor had burst into cheers the instant that the Pilot announced their independence. Chi'd been so excited by it all, only to have Randal follow xem out of work, up to the surface and then out into the vineyard until he could get Chi alone.

Again.

Xe couldn't count how many times Randal had done that. It was the most annoying thing in the universe. The most terrifying. He was big, unapologetic and completely intent on getting in Chi's pants, no matter what Chi had to say about it.

He wanted to fuck Chi.

No.

Rape.

What he'd wanted was rape. Period, end of discussion, outright. Station Master Narang had said so. Said that she'd been through it, both the stalking and the actual rape. Which, wow. Chi couldn't imagine anyone brave enough to do that to Station Master Narang. Captain, actually. Her title was Captain now.

Chi tucked xyr knees to xyr chest, wrapping xyr arms around them. What must it be like, to have that much power? To be able to look someone in the eye and know that they couldn't hurt you? It didn't make sense. Xe couldn't imagine it.

Every member of Chi's family had done their best to make sure xe never stood against them. Yelling, beating, all sorts of snide comments. It was the comments that hurt the worst. A bruise was there and then gone after a few hours. Yelling? Scary while it happened but then it was done and Chi could move on. The snide comments ate away at xyr confidence even now, hundreds of thousands of miles away from xyr family.

Xe'd run away, gone to Station Eleven just before the vote to leave Old Earth's system. And then xe'd spent the next year hiding from everyone who might report back to xyr family where xe was so that xe wouldn't be sent home.

Home.

That hadn't been a home. It was hell and Chi was so glad to be free of all of them. Especially Mom with her arch looks, snide comments and never-ending hums of disapproval before she ordered Chi to do things xe didn't want to 'for the family's sake'.

New Hope, as Station Eleven had been renamed once the engines were on, had been Chi's great hope of a new beginning. A new life with no one who knew about xyr past. Xe could start over, get a proper education instead of the slapdash one xe'd gotten and then work xyr way up into being someone important.

Like Captain Narang.

Chi just had to figure out how to deal with Randal and his stalking. If he came back. No, he was sure to come back. Unless Captain Narang actually did space him, Randal would be back with his comments and touches and creepy insistence that xe loved him despite Chi loathing him.

Xyr doorbell chimed.

Chi yelped and scooted away from the door, heart pounding. The second chime got xem back to xyr feet. The security pad showed Sushila Vlahovic, Randal's twin sister, along with Efemena and Xue, both of whom looked terrified. Their fear got Chi to open the door.

"You have to come quick!" Sushila said the instant Chi's door slid open. She grabbed Chi's arm, trying to drag xem right out of xyr rooms. "They've arrested Randal. You've got to get them to back off and let him go, Chi!"

Chi jerked xyr arm free. "No."

Sushila's eyes went narrow even though her hands fluttered like she was frightened. The way her lips narrowed and her chin came up reminded Chi so much of xyr mother. Had xe never noticed that Sushila was like Mom? Maybe. But Chi'd always been twice as wary of Sushila as xe was of Randal so maybe xe had noticed, just not consciously.

"What do you mean, no?" Sushila demanded. "They said he's charged with stalking and rape threats. You have to testify that he'd never do something like that, Chi!"

"That's exactly what's he's been doing to me and I mean no," Chi replied as firmly as xe could even though xyr hands were shaking. And xyr knees. "Captain Narang caught him stalking me out in the vineyard and escorted me back to report him. I'm not doing anything that lets him come back and keep bothering me."

"Chi!" Sushila snapped.

The sheer fury on her face drove Chi's stomach right up her throat. Acid burned at the back of her mouth as Sushila grabbed Chi's wrist hard enough that the bones gritted against each other. No way could Chi pull free from that. Sushila was as tall as Randal, nearly six foot, and Chi was barely five.

"You don't mean that," Sushila said and no, it wasn't a comment. It was an order, a threat that if Chi didn't obey there'd be consequences. "Now stop being stupid and come on. They're talking about spacing Randal if their investigation turns up anything."

"Let me go!" Chi screamed so loudly that both Efemena and Xue skittered backwards.

Xe flailed xyr free arm out, slapping the security panel as xe screamed and struggled, kicking at Sushila even though xyr legs were too short to connect. Sushila snarled at xem, dragging xem away from xyr rooms despite the way Chi fought, despite Xue sobbing, despite Efemena catching Sushila's shoulder to try to stop her.

"Someone help!" Chi screamed and screamed and screamed while Sushila cursed at xem for being stubborn and stupid.

It didn't matter what Chi did. Sushila was bigger and stronger and lots meaner. Xyr feet skidded across the ground, kicking up bits of gravel and dirt. Once Sushila dragged xem onto the grassy path Chi lost all traction, tumbling to xyr knees.

Sushila grabbed the back of Chi's pants and hauled xem upright, shoving xem towards the security station. "Quit resisting! You'll do as you're told, you stupid child. Randal wants you so he gets you."

Chi stumbled from the force of the shove, throwing xyr arms out to keep from falling flat on xyr face. Xe scrambled in the grass, up again as someone grunted. There was a thud and a groan before Chi could whirl around.

Purdie Tosi stood over Sushila's unconscious body, panting with xyr hands in fists. "You all right?"

"I... maybe?" Chi said.

And then burst into tears because someone had helped. Purdie looked so horrified by the tears that Chi waved a hand. Xyr legs gave out underneath xem, dropping xem back to the grass. As Purdie stood guard over Sushila, Xue ran over to hug Chi. Then Efemena came to hug them both.

"Why would she do that?" Xue whispered. "Why did she treat you that way?"

There was shouting in the distance, from the security station, along with whistles and the whine of hoverboards. Chi couldn't manage words. All xe could do was pat Xue's back while struggling to control xyr breathing. Xue was tiny and bony in Chi's arms. Efemena was soft and warm against Chi's back.

"What's going on?" Zhi Meeuwis, the exact same security guard that Chi had reported Randal to asked as he strode up to them. "Oh, hell, kid. You all right? What happened?"

"Randal's twin sister," Chi managed to say even though she had the hiccups mixing with her breathless sobs. "Wanted me... wanted me to recant. To get him out. Said he wants me so he gets me."

"She was dragging Chi away," Purdie explained. "Chi was screaming at the top of xyr lungs. Both Xue and Efe tried to stop Sushila but she wouldn't listen. So, I ran downstairs and decked her."

"Whole family's gonna get themselves spaced at this rate," Zhi grumbled. "Right. Good job, kid. You got an excellent punch. Head back home, Chi. I'll be back to collect your statement, all of your statements, once I get this one secured next to her brother."

Zhi hefted Sushila up over his shoulder easily even though she was much taller than he was. He carried her off towards the security station, already calling in the incident. Chi heard him call it a continuation. Not a separate incident but a continuation of what had already happened to Chi.

"Can you stand?" Purdie asked so nervously that Chi nodded automatically.

"Thank you!" Efemena said.

She got to her feet and darted over to hug Purdie tightly. That made Pudie's cheeks go so red that Chi smiled. Xe patted Xue's back again, then got both of them to their feet, even though Xue was shaking as hard as Chi was.

Xyr arm hurt. It wasn't just bruised. It really, really hurt. As in swelling and xyr fingers weren't working and the pain was ridiculous now that Chi wasn't quite so panicked. Chi bit xyr lip just outside xyr rooms. The entire apartment building was watching them. Every single balcony had someone on it but only Purdie, Xue and Efemena had done something about it.

"I think I need to go to the hospital," Chi said as xe cradled xyr arm to xyr chest.

"That does look broken," Xue agreed. She wiped her cheeks and shook her head when Chi couldn't move her fingers. "Yeah, broken. Best to get it set properly before the nanites heal the bone wrong. We'd best hurry."

"I'm getting a flyer," Efemena said. "Purdie, you call in that we're going to the hospital with Chi. Xue, keep Chi as calm as you can. I know, I know."

She ran off before Chi could say that xe was calm now. It was a lie so that was probably for the best. Chi ducked into xyr rooms to avoid all the eyes on xem. Purdie went, too, using Chi's security pad to inform Zhi that they'd be at the hospital for the foreseeable future.

The way that they closed ranks around Chi felt so strange. It was weirder than Sushila's attack, stranger than Captain Narang saving her out in the vineyard. Having anyone on Chi's side felt weird.

Nice, but weird.

Chi let them wrap xem up in a soft old cardigan that Efemena had left the last time they'd had a group dinner. Then let Xue and Efemena bundle xem into a flyer, let Purdie fly them off in the opposite direction to the closest urgent care center. Not the proper hospital that was beneath their feet, under the water layer and built into the hundred feet of regolith that made up the hull of New Hope. Probably better to go to urgent care anyway. It wasn't that bad.

Hopefully.

Except they got one scan of Chi's arm and then they were all shuffled into an elevator that took them straight down to the urgent transit system to the hospital. Chi bit xyr lip as the nurse on the transport started attaching monitors to xyr arm, chest and earlobe.

"It's not that bad, is it?" Chi asked.

"It's a really bad break, dear," the nurse said. "You and your family are all shaken up, too. Best to have you all checked out. We'll probably keep the lot of you overnight. I've already called to inform your supervisors of the incident. You'll not be expected at work tomorrow. Not that most places will be open for work tomorrow. Freedom Day, you know."

The nurse grinned and patted Chi's shoulder gently before hurrying off to take care of a tiny baby who was crying like xyr lungs were full of fluid. Poor baby.

Not that Chi could really focus on the baby.

Family.

The nurse had called Xue, Efemena and Purdie Chi's family. That was…

Something.

Chi wasn't sure what to make of that. All of xyr experiences with family had been so bad. Sure, xe trusted Xue. Xe loved Efemena's hugs and cooking. Purdie was strong and shy and sweet as could be. But family? That was… Chi wasn't at all sure about that.

2. EFEMENA MAC DIARMADA

The hospital smelled of antiseptic. Chi never had liked that smell. It was tied to so many instances of xyr family beating xem up. Or each other. Or someone else, someone not related to them. Acid burned at the back of Chi's throat for the second time. It took both Xue and Purdie helping for Chi to manage to get off the transport and into the wheelchair the hospital nurses had waiting for xem.

"Sorry," Chi said. Xyr voice came out so hoarse that Chi was astonished when Efemena nodding.

"It's okay, Chi," Efemena said. "We all know you've got issues with hospitals."

"How?" Chi groaned.

Efemena grinned at xem. "Chi. Seriously? You avoid even being in the same district as a hospital. I walked an extra three miles with you one day just so that you could avoid the entrance to the hospital."

"...That doesn't mean anything," Chi protested even though xe was blushing.

Xe hadn't realized that it was that obvious. Darn it. Not that Chi had much time to think about it because they were out of the receiving area and into a treatment room right then. Xue was gestured to a seat. Purdie was scanned and then sent to sit with Xue who'd started crying again. Efemena, though, stuck right by Chi, answering all the questions that sounded like random noise to Chi.

"No, Chi's reported her," Efemena said as the doctor, a little old woman with bone-white hair piled up in a huge knot of dreadlocks on the top of her head. "Actually, I think Chi reported both Sushila and Randal."

"Well, I should hope so," the doctor huffed as she ran a scanner over Chi's arm. "This is badly broken. We'll need to work intensely with the nanites to get all the bone fragments into position. Have they properly blocked the pain for you, dear?"

"Um, it hurts?" Chi said, staring at the doctor and then at Efemena because blocked the pain?

"Chi avoids doctors," Efemena said with a tired sigh. "Xe probably need to have xyr nanites tuned. I don't think xe's ever sat still long enough to have it done."

"Ah," the doctor said.

Her lips went thin but she didn't say anything else. She didn't even look angry about having to do extra work. Not that it mattered. Chi's heart was already pounding because xe'd messed up and xe was going to get in so much trouble over this. Xe just knew it.

Then Efemena enveloped Chi in a hug, carefully avoiding xyr arm. "It's okay, Chi. It's okay. I've got you. We've all got you. Come on. Lean back against me and let Doctor Akira work."

"You know her?" Chi asked as xe tried to do it.

It was so hard to lean back but turning away from Dr. Akira and into Efemena's soft, comforting embrace made it easier. Better. Dr. Akira gently arranged Chi's arm on a support pad with a pillow covered with computer interfaces.

That was as much as Chi saw because Efemena gently turned xyr face back into xyr shoulder.

"I do," Efemena said in her so soothing, deeper tone of voice, the one she used when dealing with crying little kids. "Dr. Akira is the one I told you guys about who's been helping me with little Channing at the kindergarten. He's so terrified of everything and everyone but Dr. Akira's gotten him to laugh twice and he's willing to let her touch him without all sorts of elaborate precautions first. She's awesome. She'll take care of you and we'll be headed home in no time."

"Well, that I can't promise," Dr. Akira said. She chuckled at both Xue and Chi's whines. "Your nanites do need a full system update, Chi. That's going to take all night. And the repositioning of your bones plus the fusing of them will take at least until the small hours of the morning. But we'll get the four of you into a group bedroom once I've got the process started. I do need to get brace material for your arm. Stay right there and don't move."

Unfortunately, Dr. Akira didn't have to leave the room. She went to a cabinet on the wall, rifling through it until she found some purple putty in a head-sized bin. Chi shook xyr head violently. Not that. Not that stuff! Just seeing the bin had Chi gagging and shaking and trying to climb right off the bed even as Efemena gently, carefully, restrained her while making shushing noises.

"Not purple?" Dr. Akira asked as if she was used to people having a panic attack at seeing the stuff. "Well, we've got scarlet, green and white. Which is better?"

"W-white," Chi said. Xyr voice came out shaky and terribly hoarse but neither Efemena nor Dr. Akira commented on it.

"We'll put it on cold," Dr. Akira announced, much to Chi's confusion.

Every time Father had broken xyr bones in the past, the putty had been hot to the touch. It'd all but branded xyr skin. The doctors had always said that it helped the nanites work, that it encouraged blood flow and healing, but Chi hated it. Father would grab xyr arm or leg or cheek or whatever and squeeze, reminding xyr to keep xyr mouth shut. The heat intensified so much whenever he did it that Chi whimpered as Dr. Akira pulled out some of the white putty and smoothed it over xyr arm.

"Cold!" Chi squeaked. Xe stared at xyr arm.

"Yep," Dr. Akira said. She grinned at Chi. "Always had the hot application before, I'd guess. It's generally recommended but not required. This will cycle in temperature over the next forty-eight hours, half an hour cold, half an hour hot. The combination is much better in my opinion. Reduces swelling and encourages blood flow. Does take a bit more work to mold it to shape if you're in a hurry but we're not so I can just smooth this on and let it naturally take shape around your arm."

She did make sure that Chi's fingers were positioned correctly, putting little metal braces under each to hold them where she wanted. Then she left the putty to slowly drift up over Chi's arm and hand. While Dr. Akira hummed, murmuring things over her pad in Japanese that Chi didn't understand, the white putty crept and cradled, drifted and puddled, all around xyr arm.

The cool was soothing. So soothing. Chi relaxed as xyr arm was cocooned in ice-white putty that slowly went rigid.

"There we go," Efemena murmured once Chi's purple fingers were covered by the putty. "See? She's amazing, isn't she?"

"Mm-hm," Chi agreed.

Whatever Dr. Akira was doing on her pad, it made a huge difference on the pain, too. Or the white brace did it. Chi couldn't tell. All xe knew was that the pain from the break subsided until it was the dullest of throbbing aches, distant enough that Chi found xemself drifting off towards sleep.

Still cuddled in Efemena's arms.

That was... odd? Well, no, not odd. It was nice. Efemena always gave the best hugs out of anyone Chi had ever met. That she seemed to like giving hugs to Chi just as much as to Purdie and Xue was odd. And that she was completely comfortable sitting there like a human pillow for Chi to curl up against was very strange.

Not strange enough to keep Chi awake. Xe woke maybe an hour later as xyr brace heated to the point that it felt uncomfortably warm. Not as hot as the purple braces that Chi was used to but still hot. Like the temperature of tea when it was too hot to drink still instead of the near-burning temperature of forged metal that'd cooled to the eye but was still hot to the touch.

"Hey," Efemena murmured when Chi shifted. "You ready to go to the other room? Purdie and Xue fell asleep already but they kind of want to move us soon."

Chi started. Purdie was cuddling Xue just the same way that Efemena had Chi in her arms. The pain in Chi's arm was so low that xe started to push xemself away only to freeze when there was a spike from xyr wrist.

"No using it yet," Efemena warned. She caught Chi's upper arm, keeping xem from moving too much as she sat up with Chi still held close. "Dr. Akira said that you've got several days of healing to go before you can use your arm even a little bit. Your boss called and left a message. None of us knows your security code so we don't know what he said."

"Oh no," Chi whispered as she fumbled with her pad.

It was the cheapest pad you could get, floppy and thin, intended to be disposable after a dozen or so uses. Chi had kept it for more than a year now because xe didn't dare spend the money to get a new one. A better one.

Logically, xe could and should. There were programs where you could get pads for free if you filled out the proper forms and did a bit of community service like weeding in the gardens or reading to kids in the library. Chi had never done them because xe was still afraid of having anyone know anything about xem.

Xe stared at the wrinkled, glitchy surface of xyr pad. "I should replace this."

"Well, yes," Efemena said. She stared at Chi, eyes wide. "I assumed there was some sentimental attachment to it."

"No, just… afraid," Chi said. "Giving it up meant… I don't know. Risking being deported, being sent back home. But there's no going back now. We're free of Old Earth. I can't ever be sent home."

"No, you can't," Efemena said in a much softer tone, one that was full of sympathy. And wonder.

When Chi looked at her, Efemena looked back at her as if Chi had just told her the secrets of the universe. Chi cocked xyr head to the side. That… How could Efemena be afraid of being sent home? Everyone loved her. No one would ever call her a waste of flesh and a drain on their finances. Chi couldn't imagine anyone ever beating Efemena.

"Sorry," Efemena said after a second. Her cheeks were very red. "I um. I've spent most of my life trying to forget that I had anywhere else to be. And now I don't. It's kind of strange."

"Odd," Chi agreed.

"That. Other room?"

"Yes, please."

The other room was one of the family rooms where an entire clan of people could pile in and take care of the sick person. The central bed was low to the floor, basically just a mattress set on the floor except that there was a jack that would push it up to treatment height and lower it back down as needed. Around the bed were wide tea couches, the sort that Muslim people would sit on and have tea while debating Islam, philosophy and science.

Dr. Akira put in an appearance, carrying a whole stack of lovely fluffy pillows for Xue, Purdie and Efemena. A nurse in a Sikh turban showed them where the blankets were before hooking a little monitoring computer up to Chi's brace.

"Looks good," the nurse said. His beard bushed out as he grinned at Chi. "The bones are settling in nicely. They should have started to fuse by morning. Do you need anything?"

"Um, a new pad?" Chi asked even though xe wasn't sure xe could get one here. Xe held up xyr old one. "My boss sent a message but this one is too mangled for me to get it easily, especially one-handed."

"Oh, wow, yeah," the nurse agreed. "That's a mess. I'll get you one that can stick to things. It'll make it easier for you to use it one-handed. Big or small?"

"Oh, pocket-size?" Chi suggested even though xe felt bad putting any sort of requirements on the poor nurse. "Any old thing will work. But pocket-size would be easier to carry about."

"We got lots of pocket pads," the Nurse said with another of his beard-bushing grins. "We go through so many of them that we buy them by the box. I'll be right back."

He strolled out, taking Chi's pad with him. A minute later, no more, he was back with a new, sturdy little pad that looked like it would survive anything short of falling out of xyr pocket into a pot of molten metal at the foundry. Then he closed the door and left them all alone again.

3. XUE LUNGU

*C*hi woke curled around Xue.

Xe blinked the sleep out of xyr eyes and tried to figure out just how Xue had ended up in xyr bed. Xue had her own bed. Her own rooms in the apartment building. There was no reason for…

Then Chi realized that Purdie was on Xue's other side and Efemena was sprawled on the other side of Purdie, snoring softly while taking up approximately three-quarters of the big family bed at the hospital. Chi raised xyr head and had to swallow a laugh because Efemena was actually sleeping half on the floor, one arm and leg on the cool tiles while her torso and head, plus the other limbs, were properly on the bed.

"Mm?" Xue murmured.

She went stiff, then stared into Chi's eyes with fear for a long moment. That fear looked as old as Chi's fear of hospitals so Chi stayed still until the fear faded enough for Xue to find the current moment. Then she frowned.

"Efemena's half out of the bed," Chi whispered.

"No," Xue breathed.

She squirmed until she could roll over and peek without waking Purdie up. Then she leaned back against Chi's chest, muffling her giggles with both hands. The careful squirming hadn't disturbed Chi's arm at all, even though the white brace had to be making xyr arm uncomfortably heavy against Xue's hip.

"What time is it?" Xue asked.

"Um." Chi frowned.

There was light coming through the curtains over the window so it was morning, at the least. The door to their room sealed tight enough that the noise of the hospital didn't really get through. And none of the monitors attached to Chi's brace beeped or had clocks on them. Chi snorted and then fished xyr new pad out from under xyr pillow where it'd fallen when xe fell asleep.

"Almost ten," Chi murmured. "I've got messages from all our bosses saying we're off for a week."

That was a wonder.

Xue never took time off unless she was outright forced into it. Purdie never got time off because xe was always running errands for xyr three bosses but all three of them had given xem a full seven days of paid time off. It wasn't too much of a surprise that Efemena's boss had insisted that she stay home to take care of 'her family'. Efemena worked with little kids and her boss was one of the nicest people that Chi had ever met.

No, the real surprise was that the foundry had agreed to let Chi have a full week off instead of having xem come in and work admin until xyr arm healed up all the way. Xue read the messages with Chi, using her finger to scroll them up and down, to click on them, because Chi only had one working hand which was busy holding the new pad.

"Trial," Xue whispered when they got past all the well wishes and down to the messages from public security. "Oh, my. Zhi's gotten both Randal and Sushila into the justice system already? How in the universe did he manage that?"

They shared a wide-eyed look. Honestly, Chi hadn't expected that either Randal or Sushila would face real consequences for what they'd done. Randal's behavior was so very common back home. It was common on New Hope, too, though most men had more sense than to be as obvious about their lack of respect for people. Where Randal was openly dismissive of anyone who disagreed with him, most of the men Chi knew would just whine and complain until they got their way. It was like being around the toddlers that Efemena handled at the kindergarten.

And Sushila, that was amazing. Maybe not amazing given how badly broken Chi's arm was. Xe had been assaulted pretty severely and Sushila was trying to get Chi to recant xyr report on Randal's stalking. So yeah, a real crime there.

"Stalking is a real crime," Chi whispered to Xue after a second where xe realized that xe was judging Sushila much more harshly than Randal.

"Mhm," Xue agreed. "It is. A very serious one."

"I'm messed up," Chi admitted in an even quieter whisper into Xue's wonderfully smooth black hair.

Xue snorted and then giggled, turning carefully in Chi's arms so that she could meet Chi's eyes. "We all are. It's okay. Need help going to the bathroom?"

Chi hadn't even thought about it until Xue mentioned it but the instant she did, yes. Very much so. Immediately or sooner. So, Chi nodded while carefully easing back enough that Xue could slip over xyr hip to support Chi's arm as xe tried to stand up. In the end, after two attempts to push xyr way upright without waking the others, Xue had to get under Chi's arm and basically pull xem up off the floor.

They could have raised the bed to an easy standing height but that would've made Efemena roll off the bed or strained her arm and leg so Chi didn't suggest it. Neither did Xue, though she giggled as she helped Chi get xyr balance. Then it was easy enough to make xyr way to the little bathroom tucked in the corner of their room.

Business done, Chi stared at xyr reflection. Someone had gotten a blow to Chi's face during the struggle. Chi had no idea who or when. There was a fading bruise on xyr jawline that looked like it had been as big as a man's fist at one time. Now it was just yellow and green mottling along xyr chin and down xyr neck. The nanites were working well if xyr bruises faded that fast. Good to know.

Chi frowned and then slipped out of the bathroom to Xue's side. "I want to ask a question of the nurses."

"Let's go," Xue said so willingly that Chi blinked. "Not going anywhere alone yet. We promised the nurses that you wouldn't."

"Oh."

There wasn't much to say to that, at least not anything that Chi was willing to allow past xyr lips, so Chi just nodded. The hallway was busier than Chi expected, people passing by as if they had places to be very soon. But no one was shouting or running. There were no smells of blood or the stink of excrement that hadn't been cleaned up quickly enough.

Much better than the hospitals back home though there was still that horrible smell of antiseptic in the air.

Chi took a deep breath and cradled xyr arm to xyr chest before heading up the hallway with Xue by xyr side. The nurses' station was an open office-lounging area with comfortable couches for the nurses to sit on, both portable and mounted pads for them to monitor the patients, and a buffet full of food that made Chi's stomach rumble. There wasn't anyone there, just a lump of blankets and the tempting food.

"You're up!" Dr. Akira exclaimed from underneath the bright red fleece blanket that had all but cocooned her. She grinned and shook the hooded bit back. "Looking much better, too. The others still asleep, dear?"

"Um, yes," Chi said. "Xue and I woke up just a few minutes ago. I ah, had a couple of questions."

"Ask away," Dr. Akira said. She must have waved a hand grandly inside of her blanket cocoon because it shifted but Chi couldn't tell exactly what that was supposed to mean. "I'm taking a break and getting some rest but sleep just isn't happening for me right now. Too excited about everything. Questions would be good. Might distract me enough that I calm down."

Xue giggled into Chi's shoulder. It was incredibly tempting to laugh, too, because that was such nonsense. Dr. Akira looked bright-eyed and wide awake. How she was supposed to sleep when she was so aware was the question.

"Um, first," Chi said as xe considered which to start with, "I work in the foundry. In smelting. We're all getting burned all the time, just little ones. I noticed that I have a bruise on my chin that's healing remarkably quickly. Will the little burns heal that way, too?"

"They can," Dr. Akira said. A hand appeared out of her cocoon, gesturing for Chi to come sit next to her. "We can set up your nanites to respond to whatever your common injuries are and deal with them promptly. I'll give you a quick scan and add that command to the codes we uploaded to your nanites' control systems."

While curling up with Xue at xyr back wasn't quite as comforting as with Efemena, simply because Xue was much smaller and much bonier, it was wonderful to have someone there for support. Both physically and emotionally. Making xemself actually ask the next question was harder than Chi expected.

Xe watched Dr. Akira hum and tap on her pad, still wrapped up in the blanket. She didn't comment on how fast Chi's heart was pounding or the way xyr free fingers trembled. Xue, though, hugged Chi tightly around the waist and set her chin on Chi's shoulder.

"So, we have a full seven days off," Chi said finally. "All four of us. I wasn't sure if that was our bosses getting together to conspire or public security or you or what."

"Bit of public security and a bit of us," Dr. Akira admitted with a wink. The blanket shifted in a shrug that nearly enveloped her entirely. "The trials will be soon. Zhi Meeuwis did inform both us and all your bosses that you'd be required to provide depositions, all of you. Since you're family. And I did make a point of informing every single one of your workplaces that the four of you'd been through a hugely traumatic experience."

She nodded once before pulling her pad back inside of her fleece cocoon. Dr. Akira's eyes were far more serious despite how silly she looked. And how comfy. The blanket was one of the truly thick ones that would keep you so warm that you sweated through it. Or that would warm you even if it was soaked in ice water before wrapping up in it.

"This was traumatic, Chi," Dr. Akira continued in a much more somber tone of voice. "We've made sure that all four of you had your nanites updated to help you deal with the situation. You'll find yourself less prone to trauma responses. I'm pretty sure that you won't have additional triggers or nightmares about it all. But to ensure that the adjustments take full effect, you do need a solid seven days off from your normal routine. The nanites will work best with disrupted routines so that they don't have to battle against habitual emotions and responses."

"I... don't understand that at all," Chi admitted after staring for a good several seconds too long.

Xue laughed, honestly laughed, next to Chi's cheek. "I can explain."

"Oh good, please do," Dr. Akira said with a bounce that made her blanket hood flop right over her face. "Ack!"

As she flailed against the blanket, Xue pulled back enough that Chi could turn to face her. Xue's expression was calm, focused, the one Chi saw when Xue was focused on her auditing. Maybe this was part of her auditing? Knowing about things like nanites and trauma responses?

"When a brain experiences a trauma, it's encoded differently from a regular memory," Xue explained. Her eyes were all for Chi, not for Dr. Akira's fumbling and muttering. "Without treatment and counseling, a brain will sometimes have triggers associated with the memory of the event. And we all have habits of thought and action. Trauma can dig those habits into something almost unbreakable, causing persistent anxiety and panic attacks and depression. So, what Dr. Akira did was give our nanites programming to help us not get stuck in any past or present trauma."

"Not as good for past trauma as current ones." Dr. Akira huffed as she threw off the blanket entirely. She was still fully clothed, other than her shoes. "I mean, it can help, especially with proper counseling which I fully recommend for all four of you. But it'll mostly help you guys against what just happened."

"Oh."

Chi breathed slowly while rubbing xyr fingers over the lightly pebbled surface of xyr brace. That was different. All the previous braces had been smooth to the touch. Maybe another thing that Dr. Akira had done to help? No, that wasn't an important question, not now. Someday, perhaps, Chi would ask but not today.

"Can we get some food?" Chi asked instead. "Or go home? Because I'm starving and I know the others have to be, too."

4. PURDIE TOSI

*T*he doorbell chimed. Chi abandoned xyr efforts to open the leftovers that Efemena had pressed into Chi's hand last night after they'd all gotten together to discuss exactly what they'd said for their first depositions. As tasty as they were, Chi just couldn't get the lid open with only one hand.

Purdie was at the door, humming as xe rocked on xyr toes and stared at the vineyard on the other side of the community fence. Xe had two bundles of bags in xyr hands, the cloth ones that Xue always used to go gather food with. Chi blinked and then opened the door, peering at Purdie.

"Hey, I brought food," Purdie said. "We're all about to descend on you again. Sorry. Efemena talked to Dr. Akira again and she says that we should all try to do different things. And that somehow turned into spending more time at your place like we always do."

Chi laughed. "Come in. You can help me open those leftovers. I can't get the lid open by myself."

"Glad to," Purdie said.

Xe had to duck xyr head to get through the door. Every

single door on New Hope was too short for Purdie. At just shy of seven feet tall, Purdie was the tallest person Chi had ever met. Where Chi, Xue and Efemena all had South Asian features and coloring, Purdie had the ink-black skin of African descent coupled with the long limbs and aquiline nose of someone from Native American stock. Xyr hair was loose looping curls that Purdie forever despaired of and tended to cut so short that the curl didn't show.

Right now, the curls were long enough that Chi was tempted to suggest dying Purdie's hair. Rainbow shades would be gorgeous on Purdie's curls.

"How much did you get?" Chi asked as xe watched Purdie unload six bags worth of food. "Why would I even need six acorn squash, Purdie? I don't know how to cook those."

"That's easy," Purdie said. "Peel 'em, dice 'em up, bake 'em or steam 'em. It'll be awesome, especially when paired with a nice brown sugar sauce. That plus some couscous and poached fish and it's a good, healthy dinner. I was planning on making that if you don't mind me invading your kitchen. Mine is so small that I hate cooking in it."

"I've… never actually learned to cook so yes, go right ahead," Chi said. Xe fidgeted with xyr sling as Purdie beamed. "I still don't know why I was assigned this suite of rooms. They're far too big for just me."

Purdie snorted. "You're a foundry worker, Chi. Of course they gave you good rooms. Frankly, this is a little small for you. You should have at least two or three bedrooms and the big kitchen. Plus a little common area for people to gather in."

"That's… what they tried to give me when I moved in here," Chi admitted. Xe blushed. "I thought it was too much. It's just me."

And it had been just Chi. Or so xe'd always thought. Xe had never dated anyone. The sheer thought of dating, of risking someone attacking xem sexually during a moment of silliness or drunkenness, made Chi's stomach roil. Frankly, xe really didn't want to have sex with anyone. Or date. Or get married.

Friends were fine. Chi loved having Purdie, Efemena and Xue around. Xe just didn't want the sex and nonsense that went along with 'family'.

"I kind of thought that was why you were in this suite instead of a better one," Purdie said with a nod.

Xe popped Chi's leftovers into the system and reheated them while putting the other veggies and carefully wrapped fish away. Eggs and fish and cheese and onions, at least eight different onions in three different colors. Three bundles of carrots that ranged from purple-black to red to nearly white.

The door chimed again, sending Chi out of the kitchen to check the security pad and then let Efemena and Xue in. They had bottles with milk and cider plus another of Xue's bags full of fresh corn that had to have come from the other side of New Hope. The corn fields on this side of the station weren't anywhere near ripe yet.

"We have the corn," Efemena declared.

"Perfect," Purdie said with xyr biggest, happiest grin. "Bring it on in. We'll shuck it and add the leaves to the recycling bin outside once we're done. I've got plans for tonight's dinner."

Purdie pecked Efemena's cheek, then laughed as Efemena hugged xem around the waist. The two of them moved around each other in the kitchen like this was something they did all the time. And, honestly? It was. Chi had seen it a million times before, ever since xe'd made friends with Efemena.

"What?" Xue asked so softly that it didn't carry over Efemena and Purdie chatting over their dinner preparations.

"Are they... dating?" Chi asked.

Xue blinked rapidly for a few seconds. "Yes? They have been for quite some time. Purdie proposed here, you know. Back two months ago? At the party where we celebrated your promotion to line supervisor."

Chi spent a few seconds blinking as xe realized that xe'd completely misinterpreted that entire conversation. Xe sighed and flopped down on the couch to cradle xyr arm while staring at the ceiling that Xue had painstakingly painted with clouds like one might have seen back on Old Earth. Xue had done that about two weeks into their friendship, without asking for payment or even accepting a favor in return.

"I think... I'm terrible at relationships," Chi admitted as Xue sat next to her. "Everyone keeps calling us a family. And I panic. But... We are, aren't we? We're actually a family already."

"That's because you're asexual and aromantic," Purdie said from the kitchen so obviously Chi hadn't been talking that quietly. "We're all used to it. Doesn't make you any less a part of the family. You just get to be the fun one who doesn't have to change diapers someday."

"That's if Xue and I decide to have kids," Efemena said with a little sniff that was the exact opposite of her delighted grin. She was deep in the guts of an acorn squash, pulling out the seeds and muck inside.

"I'm perfectly capable of baby-carrying if it comes down to it," Purdie said with a sniff of xyr own.

Chi stared at xem. So did Efemena. And Xue who leaned over the back of the couch to stare at Purdie's very, very flat chest. And very narrow hips. Purdie rolled xyr eyes at all of them.

"Yes, I'm tall and skinny but that doesn't mean I lack the proper organs for pregnancy," Purdie said. "Now get to work on those squash. I want to get the chunks steaming quick."

Chi sat there and stared. Then turned back to Xue and stared at her. It made Xue start giggling so apparently xyr persistent inability to figure out relationships and genders and sexuality was amusing instead of annoying. Hm.

"Were... were Randal and Sushila trying to get me as part of their family because I work at the foundry?" Chi asked Xue.

"More than likely," Xue said as she hugged her knees to her chest. "I think so, at any rate. That's what I told Zhi. He nodded as if he thought it was the most likely explanation. Your work there is very important. You're making the things we need to keep New Hope working. If your knowledge died, we'd be doomed. No one would be able to fix anything after a while."

That was. Well. It was an interesting idea but the fact was that the knowledge was there in the computers. But then again, if the computers failed then there might be problems. And, frankly, Chi was one of the few who had actual training in the foundry from before New Hope left Old Earth's system. Maybe it was a big deal.

"I don't want sex," Chi said.

"Mhm," Xue agreed.

"I wouldn't mind donating sperm," Chi continued slowly, thinking it over. "I've just never like the process of producing it."

The silence that met that was so absolute that Chi blushed before xe even turned to look at Xue, then at Purdie and Efemena. All three of them stared back, Purdie with a dropped jaw that made Chi whine and duck xyr head.

"I could've sworn you had a uterus," Purdie said, shaking xyr head. "Goes to show, don't judge by face."

"Very true," Efemena agreed. "I thought the moodiness was related to menstrual cycles."

"No, that's trauma," Xue said. She shook her head and

shrugged when Chi pouted at her. "I meant it at the hospital. We're all traumatized, Chi. All four of us have issues, great big ones. It really doesn't matter why you get moody or if you want sex. What matters is whether or not you want to have us as part of your daily life."

That did simplify the whole question.

Because yes, Chi did want them around. Efemena was wonderful and kind. Xue was smart, so precise in her careful statements and thoughtful examinations of things. And Purdie could cook in ways that made Chi's belly so very happy along with Purdie being the most cheerful of the four of them. Someone needed to offset Chi's blacker moods.

And maybe Chi did have something to offer to a family beyond xyr flinching, fears and panic attacks.

Not really the so-called status of being a foundry line supervisor. That was nice, of course. Chi was quite proud to have achieved the promotion. What xe had to offer that none of the others did was the apartment itself. And the potential to get them an even better one if they all wanted.

Plus Chi.

Since it seemed like the others enjoyed being around Chi. They kept coming back and seeking Chi out for dinners and visiting art shows in the apple orchard and going out to see other parts of New Hope as a group.

"How odd," Chi mused.

"What is, sweetie?" Efemena asked, words thrown over her shoulder as she whacked the acorn squash into smaller chunks with a big knife that Purdie produced from somewhere.

"You guys like me."

"You're gonna make me stare with my jaw dropped again." Purdie groaned. "Of course. Seriously, we wouldn't spend time with you if we didn't like you, Chi. Randal was a creep but you seemed reluctant to really make him leave. Sushila just invited herself into everything. Neither of them were very nice but I was willing to put up with them just to spend time around you."

"Agreed," Xue said. She patted Chi's thigh fondly. "I do like you. Exactly as you are."

Chi nodded slowly.

How odd to realize that xe'd had a family in the progress of blooming for a couple of years without the slightest clue that it was happening. Having realized that, Chi realized with a scowl that xe needed to talk to Zhi again. Xyr testimony against Randal and Sushila needed to be expanded and revised dramatically. Xe wasn't going to let either of them hurt Purdie, Efemena or Xue.

5. ZHI MEEUWIS

*C*hi bit xyr lip, staring up at the courthouse sign. Unlike most of the sites for New Hope's government, this one was underneath the garden layer. It was also under the water layer where the generation ship's water was stored and the fish they all ate were raised. To Chi's surprise, the courthouse was a short ways up a hallway from the command and control center where Captain Leigh Narang, the one who'd started this entire journey for Chi, worked.

It looked like any other office in the command center. The door was solid utilitarian steel plate, riveted and reinforced to ensure a proper seal if there was a loss of pressure. No windows opened the interior to potential vacuum, making it a perfect place to retreat if something went wrong.

Not that Chi thought anything would. The regolith that made the outer superstructure of New Hope was a quarter mile thick, built up dramatically by mining asteroids before their departure from Old Earth's system. But the engineering and forethought of the courthouse's door did help calm xem down before xe headed inside.

It took a good ten minutes to be processed through the

security procedures and then to be escorted along with several other people to the courtroom where Randal Vlahovic was facing charges to stalking, attempted rape, intimidation and criminal endangerment. Sushila had plead guilty to her charges of assault and battery, intimidation of a witness, and attempted identity theft due to her multiple attempts to set up accounts in Chi's name all over New Hope. There was no trial for Sushila. Only a sentencing which was to take place in a week's time.

Zhi stood by the door of the courtroom, studying his palm-sized pad with an intensity that Chi realized was full of worry rather than anger. How very odd. Xe hadn't expected Zhi to care this much about xyr testimony today.

"Zhi," Chi said. No response. "Zhi!"

"What?" Zhi's head snapped up. His cheeks colored briefly. "Chi, good. I'm glad you made it without problems."

"It's not hard to find once you know the location of the courthouse," Chi said. The other guests for the trial headed inside, leaving the two of them in the hallway which was quite empty for a busy courthouse. "Should we find a room to talk?"

"Oh, no," Zhi said. He waved a hand aimlessly before tucking his pad away into a cargo pocket on his thigh. "This is the only trial this week. There's no need, really."

No other trials…?

Chi stared at him for a long moment, attempting to clear that remarkable thought from xyr mind. When Zhi raised one eyebrow, Chi shook xyr head. Goodness, how odd. Xe'd always assumed that New Hope had the same problems that xyr old station did. Xe had spent far too many days at the courthouse back home, watching an endless parade of angry, desperate, violent people be paraded through.

They would go into the courtroom angry and defiant. Almost invariably, unless they were shockingly rich, they would come back out crying, broken, defeated. It was the pattern of Chi's life. Xe had watched every one of xyr relatives but xyr father and mother get arrested and thrown in jail before xe ran away. It was xyr younger sibling's arrest for drug running and prostitution when xe was anything but that had finally gotten Chi to turn rabbit. There was no one else in the family who could speak for Chi if something went wrong. Better to run than end up in jail.

That was a fate worse than death.

But here.

There were no other trails. Was there a jail? Chi hadn't checked. What sort of punishments would Randal face? Xe had been so focused on making sure that Zhi had all the information about Randal and Sushila's behavior that xe hadn't taken the time to do anything else.

Well, other than let xyr arm heal, get a better apartment for xyrself, Purdie, Xue and Efemena and figure out just what, exactly, xe was entitled to as a foundry line supervisor. Oh, and what lines for advancement xe had in the future if xe kept studying and working hard.

Having a future to plan for was very strange. Having a true family that supported xem was even stranger.

Chi wouldn't trade it for the world.

"I just... realized that I've no idea what Randal's facing in terms of punishment," Chi admitted. "This isn't at all what I'm used to from my parent's space station."

"Where did you grow up?" Zhi asked with as much puzzlement as Chi felt.

"Ah." Chi rubbed the back of xyr neck, then sighed. "I grew up Earth Orbit Station 213."

Zhi's face went so pale that Chi caught xyr elbow and guided him to sit down on the bench sitting against the opposite wall. He wheezed as he bent double and put his head between his knees. That was. Hm. Rather more extreme than Chi was expecting.

Xe thought about what Efemena and Xue would do to comfort xem when xe had a panic attack. This seemed to be one. Then xe gently rubbed a little circle between Zhi's shoulder blades. It took a minute or so before he slowly straightened up. His head still hung but his breathing quickly calmed. Quickly enough that Chi wondered whether he'd taken specific lessons on mastering emotional response.

Dr. Akira had suggested them as a useful technique for Chi to learn when they did the final checkup on xyr arm.

"I am sorry," Chi said once Zhi sat up fully. "I thought everyone knew that."

"Nope," Zhi said. His hands shook badly as he rubbed them over his face. "Just makes sense of a couple of comments those... people made about you. Called you in-system trash."

"Ah, that," Chi said, nodding. "I've heard that a million times. 'In-system trash not good enough to punt into the sun' is the normal one. Truly, I thought my accent made it obvious."

"Not really," Zhi said. He smiled crookedly at Chi. "You talk a good bit more slowly than most people here but I figured that was the autistic thing. No one else in the department mentioned it and it's not in the file. We can, um, leave it out if you want?"

Chi stared at him for a moment before shaking xyr head. "No point. I'm sure Randal will bring it up. It's not something that matters anymore. No one can ever ship me back to my family. Frankly, by this point my parents are already in jail or dead. My siblings are long gone into the jail system. No one emerges from that intact. It was why I ran. And it's why I've no idea what Randal and Sushila face."

"Right," Zhi said. He blew out a breath as if trying to relax but his hands gripped his knees so tightly that the knuckles went white. "Well, we really don't have many choices. Captain Narang and the legislature already agreed. New Hope will not have prisons. Sure, for minor offenses people will have punishments. But for big things like this? For rape and murder and the like? There's only one punishment."

"Death," Chi said when Zhi didn't continue.

Xe stared at the door to the courtroom. They would be getting ready inside. Perhaps they were already bringing Randal in from wherever he'd been stashed to await his trial. Chi already knew that Randal would be proud, angry, defiantly certain that no one would ever convict him of a crime.

In his mind, he hadn't committed one. Especially if he considered Chi to be nothing more than in-system trash, Randal would believe with all his heart that he'd done nothing wrong. Chi had never seen him regret anything he'd done in the entire time xe'd known him. He would project nothing but calm certainty to the judges.

"Three judges?" Chi asked Zhi without looking his way.

"Yeah," Zhi replied. "The courtroom will have Randal to the left, the judges in the front, the prosecutors to the right. You and the other witnesses and guests will be seated at the rear of the room until you're called to the witness stand. That's set between the defendant and prosecutor tables. It's a pretty small room. He'll be within a quick lunge of you even with the fence we put around the defendants. You should watch for him to attack you."

"No, Randal wouldn't ever do that," Chi said. Xe smiled at Zhi's curious noise. "He doesn't believe he's done anything wrong. Randal always convinces himself that what he wants is right and legal and proper. It's everyone else who's wrong."

"Damn," Zhi breathed. His brows drew together in a thunderous scowl. "I should let the prosecutors know that."

"They'll see it, I'm sure," Chi said.

Xe nodded slowly. A small room. One with only a few people. The ones who mattered were the judges. They were the ones that Chi had to convince. No one else mattered. Not Randal, not Zhi, not the prosecutors or the guests. Certainly not the other witnesses. The only ones Chi needed to focus on were the judges.

"Let's go," Chi said.

Xe stood only to smile as Zhi stared up at xem. His glower turned into a confused hum but he stood and followed Chi into the courtroom. It was small. The judges were there, all three of them. Randal was not, yet, but from the sound of the chatter he'd been called for. Zhi patted Chi's shoulder before going over to murmur into the prosecutor's ear.

Not multiple prosecutors, just one, a fierce older woman with her hair pulled up in a painfully tight bun. Her skinsuit was covered with a loose tunic, both in charcoal grey that made her look as washed out as the grey at her temples. Competent and no-nonsense. Good. She wouldn't let Randal get away with anything.

Chi sat with the other guests and studied the judges next. Two women, both younger and one man, older. The women sat left and middle. The man to the right. All three of them had judges' hoods on which hid their hair and most everything from their noses up from sight. Still, the bright lipstick the women wore was revealing enough of gender, not that it mattered. They studied Chi just as much as Chi studied them. Also good. They would pay attention far better than the harried and overworked judges Chi was used to.

A hidden door built into the wall on the left side of the room opened. Randal sauntered in as if he owned the courthouse even though his hands were secured in heavy cuffs in front of him. His expensive suit had been replaced with a prisoner's yellow jumpsuit, his fancy bejeweled sandals with simple leather thongs.

Randal's lip curled in a sneer the instant he spotted Chi.

Chi nodded back, once, slowly, with as much gravity and consideration as xe could put into the gesture. Amusingly, Randal immediately frowned and hesitated so badly that the guards had to push him to his table where the secured his ankles to the metal chair and his cuffs to the desk.

Interesting. They thought he might attack Chi, too.

He wouldn't. Chi could see it. Xyr response had thrown Randal off. He'd expected a flinch, fear and panic suffusing Chi. Instead he got calm and certainty. Every time Chi had reacted in ways Randal didn't expect he'd first been confused, then concerned, then angry.

By the time Zhi read the charges against Randal to the judges, Randal had progressed past confusion and concern. He kept glancing over his shoulder at Chi and only at Chi with a furious scowl twisting his face.

"The majority of the charges are laid by one Chi Korrapati," the center judge declared. "We will hear from xem first."

"Here," Chi said. Xe stood and bowed properly before going up to the witness stand that was set between Randal and the so-stern prosecutor. "Ask. I'm ready to answer whatever questions you have."

"Don't you dare!" Randal hissed at Chi. "How dare you betray me, you little tramp?"

Chi turned to look at him, moving xyr head slowly, deliberately. The sheer slowness of the movement drew a breath from the judges, stiffened the guards stationed near Randal. As for Randal, he paled and leaned backwards as if he'd only just realized that Chi wasn't helpless, harmless, terrified and easily intimidated by someone twice xyr size.

Then Chi turned back to the judges. "Ask. I'd like to be

able to report the verdict back to my family today, if possible."

"You heard the charges," the center judge asked Chi, her voice dropping an octave. "The decision here is life or death."

"I'm aware," Chi said, possibly far too calmly for everyone else. "It's rather novel. I'm from Earth Orbit Station 213. I'd expected slave labor in prison, not a clean and easy death for him. This is better, I think. At least it will be quick, either way."

"And if he's acquitted?" the male judge asked.

Chi raised an eyebrow at him. He blushed brightly enough that even his hood couldn't hide it. There were rustles of movement behind Chi that would, did, make xem nervous but that didn't matter. Nothing mattered other than knowing once and for all whether or not Randal would continue to be a threat to xyr family.

The questions were simple. When did they meet? Who introduced them? How long had Randal made Chi nervous? Why hadn't Chi ever reported him before?

The answers took much longer. It took near half an hour to explain how Randal had followed Chi and xyr family around an art show in the apple orchard, slipping into their conversations and persistently touching Chi even when xe told him not to. Introductions? That was easy to answer. No one had. Randal simply walked up and inserted himself in xyr life.

Why not report?

Goodness, that took nearly an hour and a half, all told. Chi laid xyr life on 213 bare. Xyr father's abuse, xyr mother's alcoholism. The slow whittling away of their family as more and more relatives were jailed and forced into slave labor for Old Earth's rich and powerful. The left judge had her hand over her mouth as Chi explained how xe had killed, prostituted xemself and joined a smuggling group to get to Station Eleven around Pluto.

Through it all, Randal sat and stared at Chi with horror. He hadn't expected this. How could he? Chi had never allowed him to know this about xem. And his behavior had certainly kept Chi from sharing it.

Thankfully, the new nanite programming was wonderfully helpful keeping Chi from having a panic attack as xe testified. When xyr answers ran out, the center judge stared at Chi for a long, long moment.

"That was horrifying," the judge said almost too softly to be heard over Randal's breath wheezing through his gritted teeth. "You're our main witness, Korrapati."

"Chi, please."

"Chi, then," the judge said, bowing her head towards xem. "The others only confirm what you've said. Captain Narang has said that she won't tolerate this sort of behavior on New Hope. You are his and his sister's only hope for leniency, if they are to get any."

"Well, that's silly," Chi replied so calmly that Randal croaked a protest. "The rule of law is the rule of law. If what he did is illegal, so be it. It was cruel. It was unjust. It was unkind. He and his sister are both terrifying. I would not want them free to harm my family or me. I certainly do not want him free to harm someone else. I suggest that you follow the law. That is your job."

"No!" Randal screamed.

He screamed and screamed as he struggled against the restraints keeping him in his chair. It was bolted to the floor. Chi hadn't noticed that before. Xe watched him, then bowed properly to the judges before going back to sit with the other guests.

Randal kept screaming, much as Chi had when Sushila attacked xem, much as Chi had when Randal startled xem in quiet, dark corners. It wasn't a good feeling. Not a bad one, but not good either.

That changed once the judges had Randal silenced with a gag. They listened to the other witnesses who confirmed Randal's horrible behavior. The prosecutor presented a very clear summation of Randal's crimes and the fact that he had refused to even admit that he needed legal representation for this trial.

"He's gotten away with it before," the prosecutor said with a venomous glare at Randal who shuddered. "They both have. It's the only explanation for how brazen they are. We can't afford people like this on New Hope, not now that we're completely cut off from the rest of humanity."

All three judges nodded before raising a force field between them and the rest of the court. There was a brief, very brief, conversation. It lasted less than three minutes.

"it is the judgement of this court that Randal Vlahovic is guilty on all counts," the center judge declared. "He will be sentenced next week for his crimes. May Allah, God and Buddha have mercy on your soul."

Chi breathed out as Randal screamed through his gag. Xe stood and bowed only last time to the judges. Then xe walked out of the courtroom as something like laughter battled with something like grief under xyr breastbone.

Free. Xe was free from Randal and Sushila, free from Old Earth, free from xyr parents.

Xe pushed all that away.

Time to go home.

AUTHOR'S NOTE: IN CASE OF EMERGENCY

*S*ometimes your family is your husband and his family, your siblings and their families.

Sometimes it's the people you find after everything falls apart.

With climate change threatening and politics going the way they are with fascist governments blooming all around us, things could go very, very bad very, very soon. An apocoalypse could happen at any time.

I don't honestly believe that all the End of the World predictions are right, though. People fighting each other for every scrap, stabbing each other in the back? I suppose it makes for an exciting story.

Isn't realistic.

When times are hard, when the worst happens, we reach out and help. Instinctively, hearts in our mouths, unsure and afraid, but we help.

That's what I think will happen if the worst comes about. Not fire and destruction, just people helping each other rebuild with whatever is left.

IN CASE OF EMERGENCY

*A*ndy opened his eyes.

The first faint hints of dawn had turned the ceiling grey. No hints of gold yet. Good. There was time to get to the radio station before his broadcast. Wasn't so cold in the room that his breath fogged into clouds of ice crystals. Better than it had been for a while. Now things were heating up instead of cooling off. Pretty soon ice might be a figment of the imagination. Months and months of no sunshine, just thick clouds and never-ending gloom, turned those hints of grey into the most beautiful thing he'd ever seen.

Other than Torres' smile.

He reached out one hand to the other side of the bed, caressing the divot where Torres head used to rest. Where it should have rested. Two years later and he still did this. Stupid of him. But the divot from reaching for Torres' hair, his cheek, the gentle warmth of his breath on the pillow wasn't going to go away.

Andy sighed and pushed the covers back. His wheelchair was right next to the bed. Only took a minute to lever himself into it and then he was off through the morning routines. Wash up and brush his teeth with the leftover pitcher of water from last night's boil. Then into the kitchen to boil today's two gallons of water on the makeshift wood-stove Spike had created for him.

One cup of hot water went in Torres' old mug, oats added to it to give him a bit of something to eat. Nothing great but hey, it was warm and it'd tide him over through the morning broadcast.

Besides, it was about all they had left for wakeup foods. Tea and coffee had run out ages ago. Juice, too. Hell, they were lucky to get anything to grow what with the weather change from... yeah. No thinking about that. He wouldn't manage to get to the radio station if he did and that was the most important thing.

About the only thing that kept him moving every day, doing those broadcasts.

He washed the mug instead. By the time he'd done that there was sunshine washing the knocked-together kitchen gold and red. Cobbled together or not, the kitchen worked way better for him than the original one that came with the house. Andy smiled as he remembered Spike's cursing after discovering that none of Andy's cabinets were handicap accessible. The renovation had started about five minutes after that with Spike's purple-painted sledge hammer knocking the cabinets free from the wall.

Andy rolled for the front door and smiled that the automatic door opener Spike created last month worked perfectly. Swung the door open just before he reached its arc and then he was outside in the grey pre-dawn.

Plenty of rain last night.

Puddles everywhere, on his ramp, on the cracking side-walks, and definitely in the street. Andy's wheels set up arcs of spray as he rolled on up the road from his house towards the radio station. The neighborhood was slowly coming back to live. After... Torres died... there were so few people that Andy had felt like the only person in the world. Now there were thin tendrils of smoke trailing upwards from a good quarter of the chimneys of houses he passed. Yards were all a complicated mess of herbs, moss and attempts at growing vegetables but that was true pretty much everywhere in New Seattle.

The soil just wasn't that good. Too much had been slicked off when the developments were created, back Before, but they were making do. Not much else you could do anymore. At least in the Puget Sound there was water. That was one thing none of them had to worry about, unlike other parts of the world.

He zipped through another puddle and smiled at the way the water sprayed.

No one else was up yet. The Penguin's dog whuffed at him when he approached her little house, same one that she'd been living in Before. None of her sister nuns had survived but the Penguin had. Dog whined quietly, stubby tail wagging before he set his head back on his paws. The scar over his lost right eye looked good, less raw. Andy smiled and nodded as he rolled past. Good. The Penguin would lose what little was left of her mind if she lost Dog.

Wasn't going to be able to go this easy in his wheelchair for too much longer. The grass and moss were already creeping over the road and sidewalks, taking back the concrete and asphalt. Not even the clouds and could would stop the grass. The moss just soaked it all up, happier now than before. Spike claimed that he had ideas for how to upgrade Andy's wheelchair when that happened. Something about big nobby wheels and gearing from an old bike.

Didn't need it yet. Not too many potholes, though. Andy dodged those easily enough. Didn't have to worry about cars anymore, no one wasted gas for just running around anymore, so he could go wherever he wanted to on the road instead of sticking to the broken, inconsistent sidewalks. They'd never built all the sidewalks required in this development. Hadn't had the chance and now there was no way it would ever happen.

He rolled up the ramp into the radio station, chuckling as Spike's door openers got the front door, the power room door, the broadcast room door for him. Andy flipped on the power, nodding as the system started to hum. Another good thing Spike had done. No more gas-powered generator. The hydroelectric one he'd rigged up to the stream behind the station worked much better. Even the batteries were working perfectly. Whole place was running nearly as well as when...

Torres.

He would've been proud. Delighted.

Andy's throat tightened.

No. Not now. The sun was almost up. He needed to do the morning broadcast.

Headphones. Mic turned on. Stack of news that the Penguin had collated for him over yesterday. Andy smiled, paged through them and nodded as he heard people stumbling in, yawning and chatting sleepily. That'd be Arvin and his boy Daniel, first guests of the day.

They smiled as they settled on the other side of the booth to watch Andy work. Arvin's face was muddy. Must've been out checking his fields of stunningly well-growing potatoes before he brought Daniel in.

Daniel's smile was a bit distant, vacant, but hey, the boy was pretty darn bright for the brain damage he'd gotten. At least it hadn't affected his memory. PHD's and so much practical engineering knowledge would've been lost if Daniel's memory was affected. None of them would be surviving half as well without him.

If Daniel and Arvin had just been closer, Torres might have...

Andy fought down the too familiar surge of misery and loss as he flipped on the broadcast signal. It should be Torres. He should be doing this. But he was gone so it was Andy's responsibility to do it. He'd promised, sworn as Torres died in his arms that he would do the broadcast every single day, come what may.

GOOD MORNING, *everyone. This is the Voice out in New Seattle. We have a good broadcast for you this morning. Let's start with the news and then we'll get to our guests for the morning show.*

The Penguin reports that we saw two solid hours with partially clear skies yesterday, news brought to us by Sherrie up on the north edge of New Seattle. While the horizon was quite brown with particulate matter, overhead the skies were a beautiful blue. She says that God has graced us with another miracle. Can't say that I disagree. Blue skies after all this time promises good things.

We've received word that a new enclave is forming up in Denver. Good for you, Denver. The mile-high city should be well above the rising seas. If you decide to go that way, do remember that high altitudes have a powerful effect on your body. Take frequent breaks, drink as much water as you can and go slow. I wouldn't want anyone to get hurt on their way there.

The former enclave in New Orleans has sent word that they've unmoored and are now working their way up the Mississippi towards New Chicago. Apparently, the storms were just too bad for them to stay in their old home. So, anyone on their way there by boat should just head right up Old Man River. Don't bother looking for their floating enclave. It's moved on and we wish them all the luck in the world getting to New Chicago.

Speaking of which, New Chicago reports that they've come up with a great new way of processing plastic back into oil. That's news that we all need and welcome. My notes say that their broadcast on the process will be on midday today, their time, and that they'll include every detail so that we can all duplicate the process.

In truly exciting news, late last night we got a faint broadcast signal from Mexico, deep in the Yucatan. Spike was able to give us a running translation of their signal and it seems that there's an enclave in trouble down there. They're heading inland, away from the rising ocean. A wise thing, I think. Spike thinks that they're heading towards the Mexican highlands but the signal was cut off before he could be sure.

The Penguin will be leading a prayer session this evening for them after the final broadcast. We invite everyone to take a moment of silence and pray that they'll make it to safety.

Now, today I have a treat for the main part of the broadcast. Arvin is here to discuss how to grow potatoes in pretty much any kind of soil and any kind of weather. He's having great success with his potatoes this year. We're all looking forward to eating them. Plus he'll have a discussion of other sorts of starchy root vegetables you can grow where you are, all of which will go a long way to adding variety and nutrition to your diet.

Then his boy Daniel has a true lesson for us. Daniel's our resident expert on account of his eidetic memory and that PHD he got back Before. He's going to go into real detail on how to filter water, eight different ways, and there'll be a discussion of how to use activated charcoal to make sure the water's truly safe to drink. So, before you get started Arvin, can you tell us how to make activated charcoal, Daniel?

ANDY LEANED back as Daniel beamed and leaned forward to start talking into the microphone. His words came out a little thick but perfectly understandable. Good. Better still, Arvin guided Daniel through the explanation and then launched into his own dissertation on potatoes and their wonders without Andy having to do a thing. Just a few hums, nods and simple questions kept them both on track for the next hour.

His hands finally stopped shaking once he turned the broadcast signal off.

"Thanks for letting us on the air, Andy," Arvin said as he helped Daniel stand up.

"Oh, no," Andy said as he scrubbed the tears from his cheeks. Never had stopped crying the whole time he was on the air. "Thank you for coming in. That's good information that everyone out there needs. Especially the filtration. Didn't know four of those methods. I'll have to use the layered fabric one for my water back home."

"I'll talk... to Spike," Daniel said, leaning on his father's shoulder and his cane. "He can do... what needs to be done."

Andy grinned and nodded. "Yeah, Spike's good that way. Thanks again, you two. If you think of anything else people need to know, let me know. We'll get you in."

They left and Andy sagged back in his chair for a moment. The Penguin was outside. He heard her blessing both of them as they left. Good. That meant he could roll over to Spike's little restaurant, get some breakfast. The midday broadcast would come soon enough.

"A blessed day," the Penguin said as Andy left the broadcast booth. Dog whuffed again but stayed right by her side. As he should with her hand on his harness so that he could guide her around. "You sounded good today, Andy."

"Thanks, Penguin," Andy said. Her habit was getting stained again. "I'll see if Sherrie can get up here and do some laundry for us all. Just can't seem to get things clean properly. All that scrubbing is hard for me. Can't do it right from my chair and sitting on the floor makes scrubbing downright impossible."

"Well, if you need the help, I'm sure Sherrie will be glad to come," the Penguin said with a hopeful little smile on her wrinkled face. "I'll add a few of my things to the stack so it's worth her time."

"Good idea," Andy said. "I'm off to Spike's to get breakfast. Keep an eye on things and let me know if there's anything big I need to do an emergency broadcast on."

"Just one thing," the Penguin said with such a bright smile that he paused, hands on the wheels. "There's a new troop of people here. They arrived in the dark of the night, pushed through to get here even after the sun set. We're blessed indeed. They have children, eight good strong healthy children. Good people, too. Not a one who would raise a hand or harm another."

Andy stared at her. That was a miracle if she was right. He let out a breath and then another as the pain of Torres not being there to see it stabbed him in the chest. The Penguin came over and rested a hand on his shoulder. Dog put his head in Andy's lap.

Dog had soft ears. Andy pet them. Breathed. Wiped the tears away and laughed a bit breathlessly.

"I'll go meet them then," Andy promised. "See if I can get their names and stories. We should share it on the air."

The Penguin patted his shoulder and smiled. "That sounds wonderful, dear. Off you go. I'll transcribe the latest news for you."

She headed back to her braille-to-English typewriter, another Spike creation, humming a hymn under her breath. Dog wagged his tail as she led her there. Andy smiled and then pushed himself out the door.

There were new people at Spike's, three blocks away. A bunch of them, all surrounded by locals doing their best to make them all welcome. Their clothes were ragged, dirty. The kids were skinny and frightened. Man in charge was a good six foot tall, skin as black as night, but he held a toddler in his arms like she was the most precious thing in the world. Really was. Sweet little baby like that, she'd been born right when the world ended.

Spike wandered among everyone fearlessly, his piercings and tattoos a call-back to who he'd been before. Now he was their resident tinker, idea man and best chef in the entirety of New Seattle. Andy couldn't even imagine being afraid of Spike though he could remember fearing him Before. Bikers. Not what he'd thought way back then.

"Who're you?" the man asked, frowning at Andy before turning to Spike who was passing muffins to the kids. "We need to worry about him?"

"That's Andy," Spike said, grinning as Andy snorted at him. "He's the Voice of New Seattle."

Andy's breath caught as every single one of the new comers turned to him with awe in their eyes. Even the toddler turned to stare at him but at least she just looked curious, not like he was some sort of savior.

"We missed the broadcast," the man breathed. He sat down abruptly in the middle of the pack of kids. "Haven't missed a single one since we found a radio that worked. You're why we're here. You're why we're all alive. The Voice is what kept us going. Taught us what we needed to know. Gave us the will to survive. And, well, a direction to go in. This... Damn it, sorry."

His eyes filled with tears that matched the tears in Andy's eyes. They stared at each other for a long moment. Andy's heart pounded so hard that he couldn't even hear what Spike said to get the man up and into the restaurant. Couldn't hear what Spike said to him or the kids or anything.

He kept them going?

It wasn't.

The broadcast was all that had kept Andy going.

It.

One of the kids, maybe five, leaned against his knees.

"You're crying."

"Yeah," Andy said, trying to wipe the tears away with his sleeve. "I do that. Sometimes. Get surprised. Upset. Happy. I cry. It's okay."

"I'm Jessie."

She stared into his eyes, hair pulled up into two adorable little black poofs on either side of her head. Her skin was a bit lighter than the man's, more red instead of blue undertones. Someone had knit her fingerless gloves that were raveling at the tips and cuff. Andy smiled and realized that yeah, his heart was finally slowing down again. Stupid panic attacks.

"Andy."

"I know," Jessie said as if offended that he'd tell her that. "Are you hungry? The new man Spike said that there's food."

"That's why I'm here," Andy replied. He patted his lap and Jesse grinned just like the sun breaking through the clouds as she climbed up and settled down. "It's time for some food."

Jesse giggled and then gasped in delight as the door opened without Andy doing a thing to it. Still a lot of awe in people's eyes but Andy found himself smiling, chatting, listening to them as they told about how they'd found each other. How they'd started an enclave in a terrible spot and then decided to move here.

New people. Kids. Eight good strong kids who looked to Logan, their adoptive dad, with nothing but joy and love. Andy ate and listened and tried not to cry as he realized that Torres would've been delighted by every bit of this.

Torres was gone.

The world was gone.

Civilization was gone, destroyed when the world as they knew it ended.

But life went on.

"You'll have to come in and tell your story this afternoon," Andy told Logan while brushing crumbs off his lap. "Bring the kids. The Penguin will love having them there and Dog loves getting petted."

"So many…" Logan's voice went so hoarse that he stopped and cleared his throat, eyes shining. "You know, Before. TV shows. They'd have the world end and… it was ugly. People killing each other. Stealing. Raping. Just bad. And I've seen that. I have. But not… Not since your broadcasts started. It's good, man. You remind us that there's good out there."

"It's not out there," Andy said and damn it, his voice was way too hoarse, too. Jessie hugged him so he patted her little back. "It's here. In you. In me. In all of us. It's easy to forget when you're grieving. All of us are grieving something. Someone. Lots of someones, really. But the good's always there. You just have to… remember it."

Logan smiled, teeth white against his dark, dark skin. "That. Yeah. So yeah, man, we'd love to see the station. I don't know that we got a lot to share but sure."

"What didn't work is just as important as what did," Andy said while Spike nodded and came around to clean tables off, giving all of the kids a hug or a kiss on the cheek as he went. "Just share what happened. It's important to tell the story, you know?"

And it was, wasn't it?

Andy had started only because Torres begged him as he lay dying to keep calling for help. To keep living even though a paraplegic in an apocalypse was sure to die. But calling for help had turned into giving help and death… just never came.

Life came.

In fits and starts and now New Seattle was a real town full of people who were growing food and making things and living their lives together. They were living again.

Andy was living.

It wasn't what he'd wanted when Torres died. He'd never stop reaching over to Torres' side of the bed. But maybe, finally, Andy could just.

Do.

Live.

Grow.

After all, Torres always said that in case of emergencies the most important thing was to keep going, no matter what.

So yeah.

Here he went. Onwards to the future, one broadcast at a time.

AUTHOR'S NOTE: UNDER THE BLACKBERRY VINES

My Drath series is filled with families. Pretty much none of them are nuclear families, deliberately. The nuclear family is such an anomaly in history that I can't believe it'll be the definition of family after humanity spreads out across the galaxy.

That doesn't mean I think everything will be perfect with bigger inter-generational family structures. If anything, the potential for drama is a thousand times higher when you have to convince your new partner's mother, father, other mother, three grandmothers, aunts, uncles, cousins, siblings, random family friends who are basically the same as family that you belong.

Of course, making it through that drama is much easier when you have pie.

UNDER THE BLACKBERRY VINES

*A*ddison hummed as xe crouched down under the blackberry vines. They were heavy with berries, drooping so low that a lot of the vines had already put down roots at their tips. Pretty soon they would have to trim everything back, much as Addison hated doing it. Made for terrible harvests the following year but being able to walk down the paths was important. More important to most everyone.

The blackberries filled the air with sugar-sweet richness. Xir nose twitched with it. Well, that and the sap that coated the vines' thorns. Sticky sweet mixed with acid burns, that was blackberry season. At least the blackberry roots did a lovely job stabilizing the soil. Nothing shifted where you had blackberry.

Of course, nothing could walk there either so that wasn't saying much.

The station shuddered as something impacted. Or maybe something exploded at the other end. Addison couldn't tell. Xe waited, counting the seconds until a full thirty passed. No alarms. Nothing falling from the sunlight way overhead.

Couldn't be too bad so xe went back to plotting out how to make xir way into the vines to get at the best berries.

Over that low vine, then crouch, push through the other three and then stand at the center of the bunch. That should do nicely. Xe'd be able to pick pretty much all the best berries that way without twisting around too much and getting torn up by the thorns.

Getting into place wasn't as easy as planning it but Addison made it without too many scrapes. Xe'd have about half an hour before the sap started to burn xir skin. Long enough for the amount of berries xe needed.

Someone had to make Caelan and Shahnaz a proper berry pie to celebrate their engagement, after all.

Ma had outright said that there was no way they'd stay together, an unaltered human and a Gensyn. Da had said, mild and calm and far too agreeably, that they might. They just might. You never knew, an outsider could learn. And of course Ba, heavy with the latest set of twins filling xir belly, had huffed and scolded them for being so rude until the babies had kicked and everyone had to gather round and feel it.

Like they hadn't felt babies kick before. Addison had done the obligatory thing, put xir had on Ba's belly, but xe'd gone to the kitchen and frowned at the supplies right after. It wasn't right, not celebrating love like that. Shahnaz had saved Caelan's life, he had. He'd saved xir and helped xir and brought xir right home when xe didn't have to do anything of the sort.

Caelan's Ma and Da had both been overjoyed to have xir home but they'd been lukewarm at best about Shahnaz. Xe thought that it was his clothes at first, so formal and enveloping. Every inch of him other than his face and hands were covered by fabric. Loose billowing fabric. Pretty, yes, with embroidery that Shahnaz was more than happy to explain was meant as prayers to Allah. Prayers for protection and thanks and lots of stuff.

As Addison picked, xe wondered if Aunt Karena realized that Caelan was looking to convert to Islam when xe married Shahnaz. Xe didn't think so. Caelan had said so, outright, defiant and angry about the limp way everyone had welcomed Shahnaz but that didn't mean Aunt Karena had believed it. Ma and Da certainly didn't. Ba had gasped, eyes wide with horror, hands over xir belly, but xe hadn't said anything else.

Xe would have to ask Sadorr about it. For a Drathanni and a hyperactive one at that, Sadorr could be very good at picking out truths that Addison hadn't understood. Yet. Usually he got it in time but Sadorr got there much faster than Addison did. Sometimes Addison blamed Sadorr's brightness on being Drathanni but right now, hip deep in blackberry vines that could tear xir to shreds, xe thought it must be that xe was young.

Too young to marry, to court someone like Russ or Leora, but definitely not so young that xe wasn't interested. Russ had gotten really tall in the last year or so, coming up on six feet tall with broad shoulders and a low full bust that complimented xir widening hips. Leora was still whip-thin but xe had put on muscle so that xe had biceps that bulged when xe lifted anything and thighs that made Addison's mouth go dry.

Sadorr had laughed, ears all floppy and muscular tail wrapping into corkscrew loops, when Addison mentioned it to him a few days ago.

"Humans," Sadorr had sighed once he was done laughing. He'd flopped down on the grass, legs splayed out in front of him and tail still loosely looped. It put his tail-hand over his rump where he scratched idly. "You're so endlessly fascinating."

"I don't see what's so funny," Addison had huffed at him. "They're both really good looking."

"Granted," Sadorr had replied much more seriously. "For human esthetics, yes, they're quite attractive. That wasn't what amused me. You should pay closer attention, my boy. Human noses are terrible but your eyes are quite good. Watch. You'll see things you've missed if you do."

And that was all that he'd say.

Fat lot of good that did Addison. Xe'd watched both Russ and Leora but neither of them would meet xir eyes. Russ turned red every time xe saw Addison looking and Leora went pale when xe caught xir. Neither of them seemed very happy about it, either. They would hurry away if xe kept on staring even after they caught him.

Shahnaz didn't run away. That was something Addison really liked about it and it was part of why xe wanted to make a berry pie for him and Caelan. All through that uncomfortable party that wouldn't turn into a proper party, Shahnaz had smiled and answered a million rude questions. He'd been gentle with the kids, charming with the Ba's, and completely wonderful around Caelan.

Heck, Addison had never seen Caelan this happy. Xe could vaguely remember being very little and watching Caelan canoodle with xir lover Storm. But that'd gone bad ages and ages ago, back when Addison was still tiny. Before xe'd even started training with knives and that'd been before xe turned six. The smiles had gone away first, replaced by worried looks whenever Storm was around. Then Caelan had gotten quiet, cautious, fearful. Xe'd been so afraid of touching anyone, even Addison and xe'd only been eight, but now Caelan was so much better.

At the party Caelan had laughed, smiled, shouted at xir Ma and then snarled at xir sib for being a jerk. And wow, Almeta had been a complete jerk, too. Xe'd said outright that

Caelan was out of xir mind to get involved with someone who wasn't Gensyn.

"He's a damn sight better than any of you!" Caelan had shouted back. "He's kind, considerate, gentle and respectful. He didn't push me at all and you're acting like he's forced me into something. Hell, where were you went Storm decided I couldn't see or talk to anyone? When xe would smack me around? Why didn't any of you speak up then?"

Addison winced, more from the memory of everyone's faces going pale and Shahnaz's tired sigh as he pulled Caelan into his arms. There wasn't any blame at all in his eyes as he hugged Caelan, soothing xir shaking, but there was so much sorrow that it'd made Addison's stomach go sour.

Which, now that xe thought about it, kinda matched how xe'd felt when xe caught Russ and Leora coming out of a cosy little hidey-hole together. Both of them had been mussed up, hair tangled and lips swollen. Addison had stared and stared and then xe'd been the one to turn and run because...

Why had xe run? Addison wasn't anything to either of them. If Russ and Leora wanted to play together they could. There was nothing holding them back. Even if it did make Addison hiss and sniffle and try really hard not to jerk around so that the blackberry thorns dug into xir skin.

Xe kept picking instead. Xir bag was about half full, a good weight but not quite enough. A bit more would be better. Then xe'd be sure to have enough for Caelan and Shahnaz's pie.

That it kept xir away from everyone else while xe let xir cheeks cool down and the tears in xir eyes go away. Xe rubbed xir face against xir shoulder, trying to blot the tears. Caelan had cried last night.

Not hard, not loud and angry. Xe'd just sat pressed against Shahnaz's side and cried silently, tears rolling down xir cheeks. Shahnaz had held xir hand. He hadn't said a single word, not one thing. All he'd done was sit and support Caelan as xe cried and then rubbed the tears away with the back of xir hand. Then Caelan had huffed, sat up straight and looked into Shahnaz's eyes.

Shahnaz had laughed, low and deeply amused. He'd stood, offered Caelan a hand, and then grinned when Caelan took it only to tug them together so that xe could press a fast, hard kiss against Shahnaz's lips. Shahnaz had gone bright red, his dark face flushing right out to his ears and up under his little square embroidered had.

Then they'd strode off, hand in hand, to get in a big loud fight with Aunt Karena.

At least Caelan had been happier after that. Not that Addison really understood what the whole crying and then fighting thing had been about. Except maybe xe did?

Sadorr had said, once late at night when Addison had stuck around their camp so that xe wouldn't have to help put the babies to bed, that growing up was a process of creating boundaries and enforcing them. A child needed rules to be safe and grow properly. But an adolescent, both human or Drathanni, needed to start making their own rules. And forging their own friendships, relationships and plans, too.

Caelan really hadn't gotten that. Xe'd always let Storm tell xir what to do. Any plans, any trips, even what to wear, it had all been Storm's decisions, not Caelan's. So now that Caelan had, finally, thrown Storm out of xir life, xe was making xir own decisions.

And Aunt Karena had never gotten that period of fighting the boundaries with Caelan, had xe? Addison paused, fingers brushing one blackberry that squished and oozed sweet purple juice at the faint touch. No, xe couldn't remember Aunt Karena and Caelan fighting. Aunt Karena had fussed over Caelan. And Caelan had dodged questions, had avoided everyone's concern, but xe hadn't fought.

So they were going through the whole adolescent battle thing over Shahnaz instead of how it should have been when Caelan was Addison's age. Huh. Xe should pick blackberries more often. It helped figure things out.

Addison bit xir lip. Looked over xir shoulder but no, of course Russ and Leora weren't standing there watching xir. Sadorr had said to watch them. That hadn't worked. But maybe...?

When Addison had run away from the hidey-hole Russ had shouted for Addison to stop. And Leora had sobbed as if xir heart had broken. Xe froze again, this time with xir hands cupping six big blackberries that were all the size of xir thumb.

What if Russ and Leora hadn't been hooking up together? What if they'd been fighting, away from anyone who could argue with them or make them stop? Or they'd fought and then just fallen into kisses and things had gotten away from them. Addison had seen that happen more than a few times with his cousins. And they'd been about the same age that Addison, Russ and Leora were.

"Okay, what if I'm being really, really blind?" Addison asked the berries as xe picked them faster and faster, dumping them without care into xir bag. "What if they're both interested in me and just haven't felt brave enough to say something about it? What if they came together because of that?"

That fit. That made more sense out of the whole thing. Xir reactions, Russ', Leora's too. All three of them were interested but none of them had enough sense to do anything about it.

"Well, no wonder Sadorr laughed until his legs gave out." Addison groaned and checked xir bag of berries. More than enough for not just one pie for Caelan and Shahnaz but a nice little berry tart to share with Russ and Leora. "Humans really are ridiculous."

Addison closed up xir bag so that none of the berries would spill out. Then xe carefully eased xir way back down into the vines, cautiously making xir way out of danger and back onto the path. Xe rubbed xir arms, feeling a dozen or so scratches that were starting to burn.

Xe'd go home, wash up, and start making pies. If anyone asked then xe was going to say outright that xe supported Caelan and Shahnaz so xe was making a pie. And if any of the littles tried to take the tart, well, Ba would have to yell at Addison because xe was going to scold them hard.

Because this evening, after dinner, while Caelan and Shahnaz had their pie together and shared or not shared it as they chose, Addison was going to track Russ and Leora down. They might not want to share but Addison wasn't going to be stupid anymore. All three of them were too young for courtship or marriage but that didn't mean they couldn't be friends, maybe date, even play together.

And when Caelan and Shahnaz got married, Addison would invite both Russ and Leora to come with xir. Who knew? Maybe they'd make a family as strong as Caelan and Shahnaz were between the three of them.

Addison was sure ready to try for it.

AUTHOR'S NOTE: RINGS OF BEGINNING

*M*oving is always a pain. Too many boxes and too many stairs. Lifting things and carrying things, the ever-driving time crunch of making sure it gets done before the deadline for the truck; moving is awful.

It's better when you have someone to help out.

Of course, the big problem with helping someone move is that occasionally weird things happen. Odd things. Promising things. Strange things?

Well, things.

Like randomly being given wedding rings for no reason at all.

CHAPTER 1

*M*inke blew a drop of sweat out of her eyes. Again. Her shoulders ached. Too many boxes carried up too many steps. Surprising part was that it was her shoulders hurting instead of her back. Or legs. Or arms. Jeez, her arms should be the ones hurting after this many boxes full of books.

But Finley couldn't carry them so of course Minke'd volunteered. Finley beamed as Minke shouldered the front door to his apartment open. The cast on his leg was probably heavier than the box that Minke carried, going from his toes all the way up to the middle of his thigh. He'd really messed up his leg with that fall.

Suman was stacking boxes in the living room. Abiodun was in the kitchen muttering as he unpacked plates and bowls and cups from their mummification in newspaper. The apartment really was a good one. Or had been a good one until Finley broke his leg so badly. He was going to have fits with the historic front steps but hey, at least he only had that one flight of stairs to climb. If they'd taken that third-floor apartment, he'd be up shit creek in a big damn way.

"Thanks again, Minke," Finley said as Minke put her box on the stack of books closest to the door.

"No problem," Minke said just like she had every single time she carried a box into the apartment. "If someone has the keys, I'll go lock the truck up. It's empty. That was the last box."

Both Suman and Abiodun's heads whipped around to stare at her with really forbidding frowns. Suman rustled through his pockets as he came over to give her the keys. For a guy a full head shorter than she was, Suman could be very intimidating. Especially when he narrowed his eyes and thinned his lips and did that little snort thing he had when he was annoyed.

"We were going to get them," Suman said.

"You didn't need to do it yourself," Abiodun agreed grumpily enough that even Finley looked at him with a raised eyebrow.

Minke rolled her eyes. "Guys, I squat twice what you do. Stop acting like I'm some frail flower here. Butch, you know. Not femme."

Finley grinned while Abiodun shook his head. Sunlight from the big bay window in the front of the apartment glinted off his newly shaven head. She'd miss his afro but hey, he could do whatever he wanted with his hair, including shave it all off. Suman shook his head, too, but he started smiling so it was all right.

"Off to lock up and then I'm heading home for a really long shower," Minke said.

"I'll go with you," Suman said. He shrugged at Minke's surprised look. "We do still have to return the truck. I'll need the keys back."

"Ah, good point," Minke said. As if she'd just wander off with the keys. She'd planned on bringing them back in once it was locked up but if Suman wanted to oversee, he could oversee. It was Suman after all.

Finley's new apartment was in a huge, lovely old Victorian on the north side of Everett that'd been converted into apartments. It was all of theirs, really, because Minke already knew it wouldn't be long before Suman and Abiodun moved in, too. They just had to outlast their leases on their old places. Four stories, big rooms with lovely windows and lots of old-fashioned charm, the place was gorgeous.

And way, way, way out of Minke's budget. She'd need two roommates to afford it if she tried to live here. But that was okay. Her little apartment on the north edge of Lynnwood was good enough. It wasn't that long of a drive to work and the police did patrol the area regularly. Her car hadn't been broken into in ages. It was fine.

"You be careful down there," Suman said once the truck was properly closed and locked up again. "That's a terrible neighborhood you live in, Minke."

"I'm fine," Minke said, rolling her eyes at him. "Seriously, no one messes with the six-and-a-half-foot tall butch with the buzz cut. They just don't."

Suman grinned at that, thumping the knuckles of his hand lightly into Minke's stomach. "True enough but a bullet doesn't care who you are."

"We haven't had a shooting down there in two years," Minke said with a groan this time. "Like crime's all that much better up here. You're not that far from downtown and you're only a few blocks from the bars."

"True enough," Suman agreed. "Still. Be careful. Let us know when you get there. Finley will fret otherwise."

Minke nodded at that. If there was anyone on this green earth that fretted worse than her mom, it was Finley. The man was the born mom-friend for everyone he met. Honestly, it was kind of nice, if a little weird at times. Having

Finley fuss over her eating enough when he couldn't cook to save his life was always going to be eye-rollingly stupid. But calling was the least she could do. Though probably she'd just send a text. Easier.

She strolled up the street to her truck, grateful that the day had gone warm and clear instead of dark and rainy like they'd predicted. The sidewalks weren't too bad. Finley's new neighbors had done a pretty good job cleaning of the masses and masses of leaves that fell from the mature maple trees that lined the street. Pretty, those trees, but man, what a mess.

"Wait!"

Minke stopped, turned and then cocked her head to the side as a really pretty, really feminine woman ran up to her. She had a mass of deep black curls all tumbled around her face, dark chestnut skin that'd gone rosy from the run and a ring box clutched in her hand.

"You're Finley's friend, right?" the woman said. She thrust the box at Minke. "Right?"

"Um, yeah?" Minke said.

"Take this," the woman said. She pushed it right into Minke's chest so that she kind of had to take it or be knocked over. For a woman no more than five five, she was pretty darn strong. "Keep it for me. Just a for a week. I'll be back to check for it then. I'll check in with Finley. I just can't have it here on site right now. Thanks!"

"But..." Minke stared as the woman turned and ran away. "Who are you?"

"Ndidi!" the woman called back. She waved and ran into the Victorian without saying anything else.

Minke stared at the door, then at the ring box, and then at the door again. No way. She had not just had someone's wedding ring shoved at her. Not a chance.

But when she opened the box it was rings. Two of them.

One was big and chunky, made of white gold with a really lovely square cut amethyst set in it. The other was a daintier ring with a smaller but very similar square cut amethyst in it. A matched set. A really pretty matched set.

When Minke pulled out the men's ring, it had an engraving on the inside. "Forever love." But it wasn't new at all. The band was covered with nicks and dents, like it'd been worn for a lifetime. The woman's ring was much the same, same engraving and the same sorts of dents, too.

"Okay, I am calling Finley when I get home," Minke said as she closed the ring box with a little snap. It nearly bit her finger, darn the thing. "That was really weird."

CHAPTER 2

*N*didi Bianchi had the apartment at the very top of Finley's new complex. She had the whole floor to herself, or she had until she started dating some guy who made Finley grumble over the phone while both Suman and Abiodun commented about what a louse the guy was. So, it made sense in a way that she'd want to get the rings out of the place. Apparently, Abiodun was quite convinced that the guy was a drug addict and that Ndidi was getting herself into trouble by letting him into her life.

"Yeah, but why would she give me rings like that?" Minke asked Finley.

"I can only assume that she wanted to keep them safe," Finley said while making shushing noises at the others that made Minke grin. She could just see him flapping a hand and then waving a crutch at the others to make them shut up.

"She doesn't know who I am," Minke said. "Seriously, Fin. How's she supposed to get them back? I mean, I could go pawn them and she'd never see them again."

"Yeah, but you wouldn't do that," Finley said.

"Finley, she doesn't know me. At all."

"Oh no, we've told her about you," Finley said. "She volunteered herself and her boyfriend to help us move. Abi basically said that no, we wouldn't let that creep in here and when she protested that it was too much work Suman sort of made a lot about how strong and nice and helpful you were. The guy scowled a lot about that. He eventually dragged Ndidi away. I'm pretty sure we're going to have to call the cops on him every few days. He's not a good guy. She really shouldn't have to deal with that sort of thing, not when she's such a nice person."

Minke sighed as she slumped back on her lumpy couch. There he went, invoking mom-friend again. Give it a week and Ndidi would be sucked right into their lives. Heck, Suman would probably start baking her a pie as soon as he had the kitchen sorted out. From Suman's pie to Abiodun's casserole to Finley's books to being part of the family, that's how it went.

They'd done the exact same thing to her several years ago.

"Well, I suppose I can keep them with me," Minke said. "I wouldn't leave them here in the apartment. There's supposed to be an inspection tomorrow so I'll have to keep them in my bag."

"Do," Finley said. "She wouldn't have given them to you without a good reason. Oh. Oh dear. Um, I better go."

"What?" Minke asked, sitting up on the couch as if they were still across the hall instead of across town.

"Abi, don't file those with the medical books!" Finley said. "They belong with the fiction books. Really, just, just, no. No. No! I can file my own books. No, really."

He hung up and Minke just laughed. Okay, Finley emergency, not a real emergency. Seriously, the guy took his books way too seriously.

She flopped back on the couch and stared at the rings. They really were pretty. It was strange, holding a piece of someone else's family history in her hand. The woman's ring wouldn't even fit on her little finger. The men's ring, on the other hand, fit perfectly. Like it'd been made for her.

Minke stared at the ring against her battered hand. The scars on her knuckles and fingers looked at home with the old ring's scars. Even though it was a chunky ring designed for men, it looked... right... against her skin.

"Not my ring," Minke muttered as she pulled it right back off and shoved it back into the ring box. "Not going to be my ring. Not proper to be playing with it. With either of them."

Didn't stop her from thinking about the rings as she made a quick burger for dinner and then curled up in bed. She could get married now. Growing up she'd just assumed that she'd never have that. Minke'd known from the time she could walk practically that she wouldn't ever marry a man.

Thankfully, Mom hadn't ever been too upset about it. She hadn't been too happy, either, but she'd accepted Minke as she was. The various men in her life hadn't always been too good about it but once Minke hit twelve she'd been five eleven and bigger than most of the men her mother dated. They'd shut up about it once Minke was fourteen and topped six feet. Even the most homophobic men had shut their yaps when the saw Minke.

Next day, Minke carried the rings in her bag to work. Her locker was secure enough. As the only woman on her crew there weren't any worries about someone breaking into her locker and rifling her stuff. The other guys had problems with that from time to time when the company brought in a sketchy temp.

But no temps right now so there weren't any stealing problems. November was end of the year, slowing down and preparing for the Christmas shutdown. Or at least that's what management always claimed. Never seemed to work out that way because each December Sales scrambled to get every single order they could into the schedule before the shutdown. Minke'd gotten used to anguished Sales cries of 'but my customer will run out of product!'

They should have a solid enough forecast to know how much the customers needed before it got to that point. Not that Minke was going to point that out to anyone. Production management already knew it, said it under their breaths every time the sales reps left. Sales management was on Sales' side.

Besides, it wasn't like they were going to listen to her. There'd yet to be a single woman in Production who'd risen past Inspector. Misogynistic as all fuck, her company, but there wasn't a thing Minke could do about it. She was already on thin ice being as openly queer as she was. There wasn't one single queer person in the whole company besides her that she'd been able to find out.

Only reason Minke was as out as she was at work was because she just was too butch to pass as straight.

Did make raises a rarity, though. It'd be nice to be able to slap on some makeup, wear some nicer clothes and get that sexy bonus the pretty girls in the offices got. Minke'd never, ever, not even once, been sexy. Big. Strong. Smart and capable. Not sexy.

"You're in a bad mood," her shift supervisor Chad commented when he came back to check on her work at the back of the line.

"Eh, just one of those days," Minke said as she made sure the strainer was working properly. "Didn't sleep that well. Makes the whole day suck, you know?"

"God, I know," Chad groaned as he rolled his eyes. "Well, take a break. I've got this."

"Nah, let me finish the strainer and then I'll go," Minke said. "Won't take more than another couple minutes."

It took less than that, more like one minute but Chad

didn't return for a solid half hour. That was normal. He'd given the others their breaks because she hadn't leaped straight on hers. But it was fine. She'd cope. Better to get the machinery taken care of herself. Chad wasn't that good back here and he always screwed things up if she passed them over half-done.

By the time she got home, Minke'd almost forgotten the rings. They tumbled out of her bag onto her kitchen counter when she rummaged for her lunch bag. Minke bit her lip and opened the box again. Just to see that the rings were okay.

They were. Of course. Why wouldn't they be?

The box sat on the counter next to her bag as she made dinner, ate it standing up and then washed up the dishes. It was there as she mopped the floor, vacuumed for the first time in way too long and then as she did a load of laundry in the little stacked washer-drier in her hall closet.

"They're not mine," Minke whispered as she folded her clothes and carefully did not go open the box of rings again. "And they're not ever going to be."

CHAPTER 3

When Friday came Finley outright ordered Minke to show up at his new apartment with beer and chips. Despite the weather coming in. Minke made sure she had the ring box tucked into her jacket pocket. She also made sure she had blankets, those pocket warmers hunters used, a thermos full of hot coffee and two sandwiches because damn but the weather had changed on Thursday. Better safe than sorry with the storm coming in.

They had an Arctic cold front bearing down on the Puget Sound that was in the process of colliding with a Pineapple Express straight out of South Asia so the weather guys were warning everyone to keep their butts securely inside where they'd stay warm. The snowfall was going to be epic.

Minke didn't really see much of a difference between staying in her barely insulated apartment and braving the quickly icing up streets. She'd made sure to wrap heating tape around the pipes in her apartment and she had the water running a slow, hot, trickle so if she was lucky her pipes wouldn't freeze. The water bill was going to be obnoxious but hey, she already knew the landlord wouldn't fix the pipes in her place without jacking up her rent. Better to get some insurance before she headed out.

The streets were dead-empty, only a few police SUVs patrolling. Her truck trundled right through the snow, didn't seem to notice the growing ice under the snow. Minke snorted as she turned onto Finley's street. Someday Everett would catch a clue and start plowing and sanding the streets before the snow stopped. Maybe. Streets wouldn't get half so bad if they'd just figure that one thing out.

But no, she saw not one sander or plow or even a deicer on her way there. Thankfully, there was a spot right next to Finley's car that her truck slotted into perfectly. Minke grabbed her blanket, her thermos, and her sandwiches, heading inside with the collar of her jacket pulled up around her neck.

Didn't do a damn thing to stop the snow from getting down her back but nothing was at this point. The snow fell so hard that she was hard pressed to see where to put her feet. When the wind kicked up in an hour or so it was going to be a blizzard out here.

"No, I am not going out there," Ndidi snapped as Minke let herself into the front door of the Victorian.

Ndidi was there, glaring up at a very white, very annoyed looking guy. Average sort of guy, short with a scruffy beard and perfectly combed hair that looked straight out of the Great Depression. Side part, square cut bangs, short in the back. Stupid hairstyle that only looked bad on a guy, never good. The idiot only had a light jacket on but from the way his hands were shaking the temperature wasn't an issue.

"Look, we need to go if we're going to get there," the guy said. He had keys in his hand, clenched tight. From the Hello Kitty charm on them, Minke had to assume that they were Ndidi's.

"It's too dangerous," Ndidi said. Her eyes barely even

flicked in Minke's direction as she tried to grab the keys out of the guy's hands. "Come on, give me my keys back."

"Quit being such a--Hey!"

The guy shouted as Minke grabbed his wrist and forced it down so that Ndidi could wrest her keys from his hand. He tried to hang on but Minke tightened her fingers until the guy gasped and whined. Minke passed her blanket, sandwiches and thermos over to Ndidi so that she could focus on the guy.

"Bitch, what the hell?" the guy asked, trying to jerk free.

"You want to go?" Minke said, grabbing him by his shirt front. "Okay. You can go. She's staying."

Minke picked him up, easy enough to do because the guy was maybe five eight and no more than a hundred ten, a hundred twenty pounds under the jacket that was puffier than she'd thought. Down lining. Good. He had enough insulation to survive out there in the snow. He kicked and shouted loud enough that Suman flung open his door glaring. Suman, being Suman, immediately pulled Ndidi into their apartment, shutting the door firmly.

"What the hell?" the guy screamed as Minke tossed him off the steps and then glared down at him. "I should call the cops on you!"

"Go right ahead," Minke said. "It'll take them at least an hour to get here, maybe longer and by that time I can pound you through the concrete. You got keys to her apartment?"

He started cursing only the scream when Minke came down the stairs at him. She caught the back of his jacket, gripped the back of his neck and then patted his pockets for anything that felt like keys. Nothing. Potential needles and a wallet but no keys that she could find on a quick check.

"Good, get the hell out of here before I kick your ass into the street," Minke said as she let him go.

He stared, then turned and ran when Minke made a fist

and smacked it into her palm. Yet again, no one messes with the big-ass butch in flannel. Just didn't happen. Minke waited until he ran around the corner, looking like he wasn't going to stop anytime soon, before she headed back inside.

"Oh my god," Ndidi said the instant Minke was in Finley's apartment. "Are you okay? He didn't hit you, did he?"

"Eh, his arms aren't long enough to connect," Minke said. She passed her jacket to Suman only to snatch it back so that she could pull the ring box out. "You want this back? I think he might be gone for a good long while."

Ndidi stared at the ring box and then burst into tears.

Abiodun and Suman swept in, bustling Ndidi off to the sofa next to Finley who wrapped an arm around her shoulder as she hiccup-cried. Minke stuck the box into her pocket and retreated to the kitchen to help Suman make hot chocolate. Or, more accurately, to hover and bite her lip as Suman poured the hot chocolate he'd already made. At least there was enough for all of them. She would have gladly given her cup to Ndidi if it made her feel better but the warmth was really nice.

Minke ended up sitting on the floor because no way was she crowding into the couch when it was already overfull with three guys patting and comforting Ndidi as she sipped her hot chocolate and sniffled.

"Sorry," Ndidi finally said about twenty minutes later. "I've just been so upset about him. He seemed okay at first but he's turned into a complete nightmare and I just don't know what to do."

"I'm sorry," Minke said and really meant it. "I shouldn't have gone right to that. I do think he's gone for a while. At least overnight. It's right on the verge of blizzard out there. So, you've got breathing room. And I kinda scared the heck out of him. Just don't know why you'd hook up with a dweeby little twerp like him."

"Not like anyone's interested in me," Ndidi said, staring into her mug so that she missed Minke's jaw dropping open.

"Oh dear," Finley said, shaking his head as he one-arm-hugged Ndidi. "You really have no idea."

"Of what?" Ndidi demanded. "Black guys don't want me. I'm too dark skinned. White guys just want a quick fuck with the 'exotic' black girl. The women aren't much better up at the gay bar. Even down in Seattle all I get are a lot offers for sex but nothing like a real relationship."

Minke opened her mouth to say something, she had no idea what, but all that came out was a kind of garbled whine. How the hell could anyone look at Ndidi and see casual fuck? She was gorgeous. Pretty and obviously sweet. Granted, she didn't know a lot about Ndidi but Finley, Suman and Abiodun all had filled her in on Ndidi over the last week or so.

"There's one person interested in this room," Abiodun said and then snickered when she stared at him. "Nope, sitting there with her tongue tied."

"Her?"

Minke groaned and flopped back on the floor even though there was a pretty serious draft coming in from the front door. Damn it. Another girl who didn't realize that she was a woman. Most of the time it didn't bother her but when she found a pretty girl and they didn't even realize that Minke was a woman, it sucked.

"I thought you were trans," Ndidi said. "I mean... Wow. I think I'll just shut my mouth."

"Don't," Minke said, laughing quietly. "Not trans. Just butch. Very, very butch. Butcher than most guys, actually. Goes with being ridiculously tall."

When Minke sat up again, Ndidi was smiling at her. A bit of a watery smile but that was justified. At least she was smiling. Finley grinned and promptly invited Ndidi to join them for dinner and then watching cheesy movies.

"I really shouldn't intrude," Ndidi said, biting her lip and looking somehow three times as cute as she fluttered her eyelashes completely ineffectively at Finley. Didn't do a thing to him but man, it made Minke's heart flutter along with them.

"Nonsense," Finley said. He waved at his cast. "I can't do anything fun anyway and with the weather, Minke's going to be here all night."

"It's way warmer than my apartment," Minke explained. "Honestly, I kind of expect the pipes to freeze even with heater tape on them and water running."

"She still lives in north Lynnwood," Suman mock-whispered to Ndidi who stared at Minke in horror.

"It's not that bad," Minke huffed.

Abiodun shifted so that he could lean into Suman's arms. Oh great. Story time. She knew that look. Finley grinned because he knew it, too, while Suman started snickering. The only one who didn't know what was going on was Ndidi and even she had that suspicious-amused look on her face that people got when they just know that their leg was about to be pulled.

"Tell the stories," Minke said with a tired sigh and a roll of her eyes. "Might as well. Not like it's all that different from throwing the dweeb out."

Abiodun laughed. "Well, if you insist. Three years ago, when the three of us had just gotten together. We are, you realize, quite gay and very involved with each other..."

He started rambling through the story of how they'd met while Ndidi watched him with fascination. Every so often she'd glance over at Minke as if trying to see how much of the story was true. No way to know yet. Abiodun tended to elaborate on different parts of the story each time so she'd just have to pay attention to make sure he didn't throw too many whoppers into the tale.

Though honestly, this one time, Minke might just let him get away with his whoppers. It was way too much fun to watch Ndidi's expression change as the tale wound on.

CHAPTER 4

Two days into Snowmageddon. Minke sighed as she stared out at the street at the front door of the Victorian. Or tried to. The snow was blowing in sheets past the window. She'd already called her landlord and nope, her pipes hadn't frozen yet. Another couple's had so there went her rent. They were all going to pay the price for that repair.

Monday morning and nope, there was not going to be a day at work. She'd called there, too, and gotten a message saying that the company was taking an unscheduled shutdown for the next three days. Apparently, the supply shipments had gotten stuck on the other side of Steven's Pass so there wouldn't be anything to do anyway. Her boss had explained the whole mess when she called him at home.

He was perfectly happy to have the time off. He had vacation pay to cover it. Minke's vacation pay was long gone and besides, she'd rather cash it in than take it. Not like she earned enough as it was.

"You're sighing a lot," Ndidi commented. "Any sign of the mail?"

"Nope," Minke said with another sigh. "Sorry. Just. Frustrated. My company's shut down for the next couple of days but I don't have the vacation to cover the lost time."

"Ouch," Ndidi said. She made a face. "I work from home so it's generally not an issue but I was waiting for some stuff to show up."

Minke nodded. She'd spent the last two nights on the guys' couch. Not a bad couch, really, but man, she'd much rather go home. What she should have brought with her was spare underwear and a couple of T-shirts or something.

"What?"

"Just… itchy," Minke admitted. "I love the guys, I really do, but I am just not going to wander around naked while my clothes wash."

Ndidi stared and then burst into the cutest giggle-fit that Minke had ever seen. She flapped a hand for Minke to follow her, leading the way upstairs. Nice big staircase. The bottom had those really lovely carved railings that came straight from a different age. By the time you got to the third floor they were much simpler. On the fourth floor, they were dead-modern looking except nope, they showed all the signs of wear of being original.

"Come on in," Ndidi said. "I don't mind if you wander around nude. It's certainly warm enough up here for it. Everyone else has their heat on high and it's turning my apartment into a sauna."

A very nice sauna but yeah, it was stupidly hot in Ndidi's apartment. For a full floor apartment, it wasn't as big as Minke had expected. Made sense now that she was up there. The apartment was nestled right up in the roof so there were all sorts of weird angles and odd windows jutting out but at least she could stand up straight in the middle of the room. Not so much by the walls but it was okay.

Where Finley's apartment had plain white walls that they were only just getting pictures up on (and only because none of them could go to work either), Ndidi's apartment had luscious rose and sage green walls. Well, the walls were sage green and the wildly sloping ceiling was rose. The living room had those beanbag couches that you saw in the mall, covered in what looked like brown suede. Those were matched with some of the comfiest looking lounge chairs that Minke had ever seen.

"Man, this is nice," Minke said. "You did a great job on this place. It's beautiful."

"Thank you," Ndidi said with well-deserved pride. "I keep trying to figure out how to put up art but with these walls I just don't see it happening."

"No," Minke said slowly, staring around. "Unless you're talking postcards pinned up, I don't think that's going to work."

Ndidi started giggling again. Her washer and drier were the full-size sort, set in a closet in her walk-in pantry in the kitchen. Nice big ones that'd wash so much more than just Minke's outfit. But Ndidi didn't seem to mind at all wasting soap on a partial load. Though by the time she came back with towels and a silky rose robe that'd barely come mid-thigh on Minke, it wasn't exactly a partial load.

"Go ahead and stuff your clothes in there," Ndidi said. "The bathroom's around the corner," she pointed to the left, "so you can shower, too, if you want. I always want to when I have to wear dirty clothes."

"No kidding," Minke said. "Thanks for this. I really appreciate it."

"You're protecting my grandparent's rings," Ndidi said with a shy little smile that made Minke's heart thump. "Least I can do. You want some red beans and rice? I've got a batch about to go on the stove for reheating."

"Sure," Minke said. "And thanks for that, too. I'm kinda getting tired of Suman and Abiodun's cooking, you know?"

"They do tend towards... fancy, don't they?" Ndidi said so diplomatically that Minke started cackling.

Fancy was a word for it. Outright ridiculously complicated was the term Minke would have used but fancy worked. The bathroom was a cozy one, just enough room for Minke to stand upright in the shower. Which had a rose curtain and a rose bathmat and rose towels. Minke grinned. There was a theme there.

Felt really good to get properly clean and not with the guy's hypoallergenic, unscented, barely frothing body wash / shampoo. She just never felt clean if there wasn't some proper suds going on. And man, it felt even better to not have to worry about the guys poking their heads into the bathroom to make sure she was okay.

Finley was a nice guy but his worrying got a bit ridiculous sometimes.

The robe was short.

Really short.

Embarrassingly short.

It wasn't mid-thigh. It was just barely covering the strategic regions and don't raise your arms or you're flashing the world short. The overlap left a stripe of her chest exposed right down to her bellybutton because her shoulders and back were too wide. And the sleeves, despite being loose, were too tight. Minke could barely move her arms.

"That's not going to work," Minke said, setting it aside and wrapping up in one of Ndidi's bath sheets. Covered everything and no gaposis. Good deal.

"Hey, you're done," Ndidi said when Minke finally emerged from the bathroom. She blinked. "Um, no robe?"

"Nope," Minke said and grinned. "I'm just too tall and too broad for that one. Nice try, though."

Took a second and they were both laughing like old friends. Minke eyed the ring box sitting on the counter next to her wallet and keys. She kind of wondered how long Ndidi would have her hang onto the rings but for now, if it made Ndidi feel better, Minke would keep them.

While trying not to dream about how that man's ring felt on her finger.

Or how much she'd like to see the matching ring on Ndidi's finger.

CHAPTER 5

*S*oup. The street leading up to Ndidi's place was soup. Amazing that it only took a week before the whole blizzard's worth of snow had melted off. Right into the leaves that hadn't been raked up in time for the storm. Seemed like every single drain on the way to Ndidi's place was clogged with leaves.

Minke shook her head. Seriously, she was spending more time up here in north Everett than she was back at her apartment lately. Maybe the guys had been right that she should try and get an apartment up here.

Not that she could afford to think about it until after Christmas bonuses came out. That short paycheck was why she was slogging through knee-deep puddles with an iron bar. Abiodun was on the sidewalk with the snow shovel, golf umbrella protecting him from the rain pounding down, but they'd found that an iron bar found the grates way easier than the shovel did.

"I can't believe you're doing this," Abiodun said as Minke probed for the drain. Couldn't be too far away.

"Eh, they're paying me," Minke said.

"I can't believe the neighborhood watch association is paying civilians to clear the drains," Abiodun said in the exact same tone of voice. "They should have their own people out here doing this."

Minke grinned at him and then grunted as the iron bar caught on the grate. Sliding it along the gutter was a perfect sounding tool. No way to see through the water. It was murky as all fuck and cold as hell, too.

"Got it," Minke said. "Gimme the shovel. This will make the whole block cleared."

It was the biggest puddle, too. Covered the entire street and had seemed up onto the grassy verge between the gutter and the sidewalk. Couldn't be good for the maple trees but hey, at least they were dormant. They might not even notice the drenching they were getting.

Minke carefully shoveled the leaves up onto the verge, doing her best not to let the water swirl the leaves right back into the drain. Soon as the first crack in the leaf cover was cleared, the water started to flow again. Good amount of suction, dragging at her calves harder and harder as she cleared the rest of the drain.

"Wanna do another block?" Minke asked once she was sure the drain wasn't going to get clogged again.

"No, you do not want to do another block." Abiodun huffed at her. "You're turning blue, Minke. Come on. Inside. You need to get dry and eat something hot."

"You sound like Finley," Mike said.

"Why do you think I'm here?" Abiodun said so caustically that Minke cackled at him.

Not that she could blame either Finley or Abiodun. The fact was, her legs were cold. Ice cold. She wasn't entirely sure her toes were ever going to get warm again. But the street was cleared and the supervisor the watch crew had sent nodded and gave Minke a couple hundred in cash for her work in exchange for the iron bar and show shovel they'd borrowed. So that was score and well worth the cold and wet.

Her shoes squelched so bad on the front stairs of the old Victorian that Minke just pulled them and her socks off when she stepped inside. Her jeans were dripping all over the mat but that'd stop soon enough.

"Go on," Abiodun said, glowering at Minke as he closed his umbrella and shook it off. "Ndidi said you were to head straight upstairs and no complaints."

"Are you guys setting us up?" Minke asked with a little glare at him that got her the most sarcastic eye roll of her friendship with Abiodun.

"Do we need to?" Abiodun asked. He snorted. "Seriously, you two are already a pair. Just admit it and move in already. You'd save a ton of rent if you did."

Minke opened her mouth and then shut it because there really wasn't a lot to say about that. He wasn't wrong about the rent side of things. And if she said anything about her completely fruitless fantasies of marrying Ndidi, settling down and raising adorable adopted kids with her, Finley would go into high gear on the matchmaking thing. The last thing Minke wanted was to drive Ndidi away.

What she really wanted was for the two of them to be wearing the rings that Minke was still carrying around.

Ndidi opened the door and sighed when she saw Minke's dripping shoes, socks and pants. "Into the bathroom with you. Goodness, I can't believe you did that."

"Got a couple hundred dollars out of it," Minke said. "Makes up for the lost time for the storm."

"Not if you lose your poor toes," Ndidi said. "Shoo. And give me your clothes. They're all getting washed. Your robe is on the back of the door."

She was pulling at Minke's jacket and then her flannel

shirt so Minke couldn't exactly stop and stare at her for the 'your robe' thing. Not that it really mattered when there was a warm shower in her immediate future. The cold really had gone straight through her.

Besides, once she was in the bathroom the robe was one hundred percent obvious. Big ankle length even on Minke plaid flannel robe fit to entomb even the biggest of lumberjacks. Minke tried it on and laughed. Jeez, warm and soft and comfy.

"Take a shower, you!" Ndidi shouted. "Go on!"

Minke did, grinning the whole time. Well, part of the time. Lukewarm water felt like scalding but after a half hour or so of gradually hiking the temperature the bathroom was filled with steam and she felt way better. There was even a set of flannel slippers to match the robe so Minke really was all snuggly once she got out of the shower.

"You had to have these commissioned," Minke said once she found Ndidi lounging in the living room with a big mug of soup. That she passed right over to Minke.

"Nonsense," Ndidi said, grinning. "I went to the Big and Tall store down at Alderwood and told them what I was looking for. That set looked the most like you so I got it. On sale, too, sixty percent off. Apparently, no one else has your sense of taste."

"I have taste?" Minke said and then cackled at Ndidi's groan. "Seriously, I mostly aim for lumberjack lesbian when I shop for clothes. It's easy, warm, cheap and men's clothes mostly fit me better than women's."

"Well, you've got that... again."

Ndidi froze as the front door of her apartment rattled. So did Minke. No one else should be coming up here. The boys were all downstairs and Finley would probably shout at Suman and Abiodun if they dared to interrupt Minke's time with Ndidi. None of the watch would come up here. They knew Minke lived in North Lynnwood.

Which left just one person.

Minke waved for Ndidi to stay put in her lounge chair before setting the mug of soup down. Regretfully. Nice and warm, looked like hearty beef-barley soup with big chunky vegetables and not the stuff you'd get from a can.

The handle rattled again so Minke took a deep breath before flipping the deadbolt open and flinging the door open. She glared down at Ndidi's former boyfriend who had lockpicks in his hand and a terrified expression on his face.

"What'd I say about you the last time I threw you out of here?" Minke asked as she grabbed for the lockpicks.

She got them. Didn't get the asshole. He bolted down the stairs with a terrified scream that was, actually, pretty well-deserved. If Minke got her hands on him she was going to pound him through the concrete, not just into it.

Minke stalked to the window that faced the street where the watch crew was just wrapping up their cleanup work. At least they'd gathered up all the leaves that had been clogging the drains. Wouldn't get swept back into the street and clog the drains again.

"Hey, he tried to break into Ndidi's apartment," Minke shouted down to the watch crew.

Their heads snapped up and then the two biggest once charged at Ndidi's former boyfriend. He struggled, kind of ineffectively, but they pinned him as the leader of the watch called the cops. Minke nodded firmly.

"Good," Minke said. "My clothes done yet?"

"Ah, yes?" Ndidi said, shaking in her lounge chair.

"Good," Minke said a lot more gently. "Look, the cops are going to want to know what your history with him is. I need to get dressed. You okay for the moment?"

Ndidi nodded but she really didn't look okay. Not good.

Minke dressed fast as she could and then shrugged, wearing the slippers instead of her still soggy shoes. At least they were old shoes, not the new steel-toed boots she'd gotten for work.

Then she headed out and helped Ndidi charge the dweeby little asshole with domestic assault, petty theft as well as breaking and entering. Hell of a Christmas present, though. The cops looked outright delighted to have him. They hauled him away as he struggled and tried to claim that he wasn't breaking and entering, that it was Minke who'd broken into Ndidi's apartment.

"Oh, as if!" Ndidi shouted. "You little ass! Check him for drugs. I know he's an addict, too. You come back and we'll all beat you up, you jerk!"

Minke held Ndidi back, with more than a little effort as the dweeb started calling Minke a fat ugly butch dyke.

"I'm not fat, you moron," Minke said. "Seriously, just get him the hell out of here."

One thing Minke could say was that it was nice to see the back of that idiot. Not so nice that Ndidi stomped her way back upstairs and Minke's new slippers were a bit damp from standing in the rain as they talked to the police.

"You're not ugly," Ndidi snarled as she didn't slam the door even though she pretty clearly wanted to. "You're very good looking."

"He reached for the insults he knew hurt women in the past," Minke said as she settled down with her soup. "Oh, hey, it's still pretty warm. Awesome."

Ndidi stared at her. Then frowned and sat in her lounge chair and stared at Minke some more. And then cocked her head to the side, making those gorgeous curls tumble around her neck which was dappled with raindrops. God, so beautiful.

"You're not upset," Ndidi said.

"Nope," Minke said around a mouthful of beef and carrot. "This is good. You make it?"

"Yeah."

"Love it," Minke said.

She ate the rest of the soup in silence, doing her best not to twitch as Ndidi stared at her with a frown on her face. Didn't twitch as she took the mug to wash it, or as Ndidi leaned on the counter next to Minke's wallet, keys and the ring box. Did twitch when Ndidi refused to even look at the box.

"Those are yours, you know," Minke said.

Ndidi twitched.

"Come on, fess up," Minke said. "Tell me what the big deal is with them. I mean, they're clearly your parents or grand-parents' rings. Why push them on me and then never take them back?"

Ndidi sighed. She finally picked up the little box and flicked it open. Her expression was incredibly sad as she ran a finger over the woman's ring. But determined when she flicked it shut again.

"Grandma said that they were for me," Ndidi said. "She and Grandpa wore them the entire time they were married, over forty years. Grandpa got the stones from his grandfather, had them set and then gave them to Grandma. Told her to give the men's ring back when she decided she wanted to get married. Grandma laughed at him and told him to propose properly. They got married two months later. I always... wanted to have them given to me like that. To have that link to the past."

Minke stared and then started chuckling. She put her hand over Ndidi's, making sure that Ndidi didn't fling the box right into her face. Looked more than pissed enough for it but Minke couldn't stop chuckling.

"Sweetie," Minke said and grinned when Ndidi's cheeks

went red, "you're not your Grandma in this iteration of the story. "You're the Grandpa. You gotta go find someone you want to marry and give them the rings. That's how it works. That's the link to the past."

Ndidi pushed the rings towards Minke only to freeze when Minke used her strength to keep her from doing it automatically. Felt automatic anyway. They'd only just met, really. Granted, hit it off immediately but there was so much she didn't know about Ndidi. And so much Ndidi needed to learn about Minke, too.

"There'll never be a no from me," Minke said, soft and shy and feeling every single inch of her six foot six. Felt kind of like her joints were on backwards right then and all because of the stunned look in Ndidi's eyes. "There just won't. But you, you need to do it because you mean it. Because you want me. Or whoever. Not because you're afraid of being alone your entire life. Save it for when you mean it."

Ndidi huffed. It was kind of a laugh and kind of a sob, tears welling up at the corners of her eyes. "I... God. Why do you make things so easy?"

"Because they are easy," Minke said, grinning now. Her skin prickled with a blush that went right down to her toes. "This is easy. There's no rush. Give yourself time. Think about it. I don't know, wrap it up as a Christmas present or something."

Ndidi burst out laughing. She grabbed Minke and pulled her into a hug that felt just about like Heaven. Minke sighed and snuggled Ndidi. She was soft and warm and as wonderful as those awesome couches of her.

"I'll wait," Ndidi said, tilting her head up so that those lovely full lips were only just a few, a few too many, inches away. "For a little bit. But I don't think my answer's going to change either. You're getting a Christmas present early if I have anything to say about it. You make me happy. I think I make you happy. We should go for it, not wait and fuss like Finley over it."

"Merry Christmas to me, then," Minke said

Minke bent just as Ndidi grabbed her ears and tugged her down for a kiss.

Man, Finley was going to have kittens if he didn't get to help plan their wedding. Minke laughed against Ndidi's lips, happier than she'd been in years. Maybe ever. Merry Christmas indeed. And many more to come, too.#

AUTHOR'S NOTE: DAY HUNT ON THE FINAL OBLIVION

Choosing which book to share with these stories was a bit of an adventure. A romance? Well, no, these stories have romance. They're not really romantic, per se. Except for Rings of Beginning. Science Fiction? Hmmm, yeah, there's a lot of science fiction in this collection, but space opera doesn't quite fit. Political drama and revolutionary coups doesn't either.

In the end, I went with Day Hunt on the Final Oblivion not because it's focused on family. It is, the found family sort, which I love writing. Not because it's science fiction or fast paced or a glorious mystery.

No, I picked this one because Esme's attitude is the most like the characters in these stories. She's a get up and go, take no prisoners, will not surrender sort of person who really just wants to keep everyone safe. So yeah, hope you enjoy the sample!

1. CHANGE OF COMMAND

The command staff offices for the human habitat on the Final Oblivion were the most butt ugly places Esme had ever worked in her entire life. Including that summer she spent processing fish as a teenager. Smelled better than the fish plant. Barely. But they were way uglier.

Scarred steel walls without a single decoration other than maps, plans and the occasional note stuck to them by magnets send every word, cough and shuffled foot echoing across the big room. A lot like a traditional Japanese office, really, all the desks pushed up together with no cubical walls or sound barriers or, heaven forbid, sound dampeners perched on the corners of the desks.

Which were cobbled together out of whatever scrap the first drew had been able to scavenge. Made for some interesting desks. The commander, sat smuck in the middle of the room where he could watch everyone else, had a proper desk constructed to proper human standards. Most of the desks at least approximated what they should be but some were solid glass tops, the heat shield kind, others metal. A few were made of Saurid shed armor plates. Those were kind of nasty, always vaguely squishy to the touch.

Though apparently they'd stiffen over time and in, oh, a hundred or so years be harder than steel. Yeah right. Like they'd last that long. The accountants that worked those desks tended to do everything in their power to work anywhere else but their desks. Meant that everyone else piled stuff on top to hide the creepy things.

Off by the door that led to the bathroom that always stank of rot, Esme's desk was a standing desk with six layers for perching papers, coffee mugs and whatever interface she was using at the moment. It was set a bit too high for her but the damn thing was stuck in position. So she had a stool that she'd stolen from the medics that she could take up or down depending on which level of her desk she was using at the time.

Right now, like everyone else in the room, Esme had her head down and her stool at the lowest position in the hope that no one would notice that she was there. Because as soon as Commander Sergey Shchurov Tikhonovich realized that this very serious discussion with soon to be former Commander Nikita Chuprakov Olegovich, always Kesha to people he liked and that was damned few humans on this station, they'd all be ordered the hell out of here.

Tikhonovich stared down his nose at Kesha who'd put his feet up on his desk while slouching so low in his dramatically underpadded chair that his back had to be killing him. While Tikhonovich looked like exactly the sort of spit and polish rule lover that Esme hated, she had to admit he was a damn sight prettier than Kesha. Slim, tall, lean muscle, Tikhonovich's hair was just starting to go grey at the temples in that distinguished way that some very rich and very powerful and very spoiled men managed.

He was about the same age as Kesha, maybe fifty-two, fifty-three. But he looked a good ten years younger. Kesha was short as Esme, balding and didn't care who knew it. His paunch was like another person in the room, big and jiggly every time he spoke or breathed or moved at all.

Right not it was shaking like they had an earthquake going through the station, legacy of Kesha's toe twitching from its perch on top of his desk.

"You actually consider this an adequate working environment?" Tikhonovich demanded for the second time. Much louder, especially in the wary quiet that had fallen around the two of them.

"No," Kesha said, blowing a raspberry as he folded his hands over his belly. Not even to still it because he started tapping his fingers against his stomach.

The damned man was amused. Near to laughing until he coughed a lung up. He thought this whole thing was funny.

Esme peeked and then pressed her lips together because, yeah, it kind of was. Tikhonovich looked like he was about to turn purple from pure outrage. Justifiable. Absolutely everyone here agreed that the habitat they'd been given was a piece of junk but no one would pay the money to fix it. Esme ought to know. She'd audited the requisition requests often enough and seen the thousand and one rejections from Earth.

"Then why haven't you fixed it?" Tikhonovich demanded. "This is intolerable. No one should have to work or live in an environment like this, especially so far from home."

"Agreed," Kesha said. His lips stretched into a twitching smile as he drummed his fingers against his belly. "Not saying anything I don't already know."

He waved one hand, looked straight at Esme. She glared right back at him, straightening up fast enough to make her spine pop loudly. Kesha grinned, chortles finally squeezing past his control. Bastard always loved to get a reaction from her. And everyone else.

"How many requests I put in to fix this place up?" Kesha asked.

"You got a computer," Esme snapped at him. "Don't drag me into your little joke here, Kesha."

"You don't get to call me that," Kesha snapped, laughter stopping as he glared and pointed imperiously at her.

"Sorry, Commander Kesha," Esme said and then smirked as he glowered at her.

Tikhonovich breathed in, rubbed two fingers directly between his perfectly groomed eyebrows and then let it out slowly before turning to smile in that so-reasonable way spoiled, rich men had when they were humoring those beneath them by being egalitarian. And it was pushing their temper to the breaking point. Asshole.

"How many requests have there been, please?" Tikhonovich asked. Yeah, his patience was about worn thin. Could have cut through flesh with the edge in his voice.

"Kesha here," Esme grinned when Kesha flipped a thoroughly vulgar gesture at her, "has turned in one thousand, nine hundred and twelve requests during his command. Commander before him had over three thousand. One before her had nine before he was reassigned. All of them have been rejected. As have the requests to be allowed to cook our own food."

"So annoying," Kesha sighed. "I swear on my mother's grave, may she take her place in it soon, there are mornings where I would kill for a good cup of coffee before I left my quarters."

Everyone muttered and nodded their agreement. Even Esme did. Never did like having to talk to people before she'd eaten. Given her problems with caffeine, Esme preferred food to wake up with. No reason to risk the headaches of coffee first. She needed a good buffer of food before she dared to drink her drab of coffee mixed in with a whole hell of a lot of chai and strawberry jam. Sometimes oatmeal, too.

"They... denied the requests?" Tikhonovich asked.

Esme's nod made him rock back on his heels. He ended up sitting on the desk closest to Kesha's when Kesha just nodded and smiled beatifically at him. Made the asshole look like that fat Buddha stature Yannick had gotten for Tovia when Tovia was little. It'd scared the hell out of Tovia so the thing sat on Yannick's desk ever since then.

"Why?" Tikhonovich said. "Why would they expect everyone to endure these conditions?"

"What I was told was that we needed to 'foster relationships with the other species'," Kesha said and yeah, there was the brittle edge to his voice. He wasn't going to stand for much more of Tikhonovich's questioning and innocence. "So we didn't need beautiful quarters. We were all, every single member of the crew, to 'socialize'. To make friends. To gather what we needed from our environment. Had one damned Earth inspector who said that he thought this," he gestured towards the room and its motley assortment of desks, "was 'most appropriate'."

"To be fair, he was old-school Japanese," Esme said. She grinned when both Commanders glared at her. "Hey, you roped me into this conversation. Don't be surprised when I keep participating. I've done more to find us edible food than anyone here other than Yannick."

"Where is he?" Kesha asked. He flipped a hand towards Yannick's empty desk. "He's always here."

"Unless his boy manages to hurt himself which he did yesterday while having a fly-wheel contest with his best friend and three Nikiphoros adolescents. They all crashed into each other. Tovia's still in the infirmary, more because he doesn't want to go to school today than because he was really hurt."

And also because it was time for his annual nanite upgrade. Esme was due next month. She always hated that. Lying there on the beds with an IV pumping what looked like mercury into her veins. But the protection against stray radiation, cancerous cells and the majority of infectious diseases was worth the discomfort. Usually she just slept through it. Tovia'd apparently decided to flirt his way through this time, much to Yannick's dismay.

Not a choice Esme would have made even if some of the nurses were cute as hell. They all had no patience for people wasting their time, too many patients and too many reports to fill out for the bureaucrats back on Earth. Never get between a nurse and their mass of required paperwork. Might get you stabbed in some very uncomfortable places with 'vaccines' but that was a lesson Tovia needed to learn on his own.

At least Tovia knew not to flirt with Esme's sometimes-girlfriend.

"That kid," Kesha sighed, shaking his head.

"You have no food," Tikhonovich said slowly. "All food comes from the aliens on the station."

"Yep," Kesha said and there was his about to laugh smile again. His fingers went back to drumming on his belly.

"No ability to upgrade your work environment."

"Or our private quarters," Kesha agreed. He snickered at Tikhonovich's look of horror. "Yeah, that room you got to sleep in? That's the most comfortable that we've got. Some of us, not me, Esme for example, sleep on leftover netting scavenged from shipments."

"Hey, my hammock's damn comfortable," Esme protested very, very mildly. "Only comfortable thing I got but it's a good one. Had to beat off one of the new guys last shipment. Claimed he needed it to take things back to Earth. Like he didn't go buy a new one that worked better than mine ever had."

Tikhonovich stared at them both, mouth opening and closing as he tried to find words. Clearly couldn't find a single one because he threw his hands up, slapped them down on his thighs and then stood. He shook his head one more time before striding out of the offices. Down the hallway towards the communications array.

Not one of his people followed. They all let him go and conspicuously made themselves busy learning their new jobs at their battered old desks. Lovely support for their commanding officer but hey, Esme didn't know. Tikhonovich had probably told them it was first priority while he dealt with the important stuff.

Like figuring out why they couldn't upgrade the habitat.

Good. Maybe he'd be able to find out why they were being made to suffer through all this crap. Esme sure never had. None of the humans here had a damned clue and the aliens weren't ever allowed into their habitat. But then no aliens allowed people into their habitats either. Just wasn't done, sharing that part of your private species business with outsiders.

Esme was pretty sure that if they did open up and let the aliens see what things were like in here they'd either get flooded with donations to make it better or they'd get funding so that the assholes back on Earth wouldn't be so embarrassed by the comments the aliens made.

Or both.

Probably both. Wouldn't take but a few donations before Earth would get their nose out of joint and they'd have proper renovations happening. Tempting thought, letting it slip to the other species, but no. Esme wasn't going to be the one to get punished for that. Let Tikhonovich beat his head against that wall. Kesha clearly'd decided that he was the right man for that job because he just sat at his desk, feet up, laughing as Tikhonovich stalked away.

2. EVENING PROWL

*E*sme loitered outside the infirmary, humming tunelessly. She should just come back later. Every time she hung out like this Tanya snapped at her and threatened to subject her to every test in the universe. Including the ones that didn't apply to humans. People lurking outside the infirmary were assumed to be avoiding treatment.

Not trying to ask their girlfriend if she wanted to go eat together.

"What are you doing?" Boreyeva Tatiana Nikolayevna, the beautiful Tanya, snapped as she glared out the door at Esme.

Not a good day. Tanya's hair was stringy with sweat. Her scrubs were spotted with blood and what had to be a crust of vomit. One of the newbies must have gotten sick dealing with the station. Or brought something with them.

"Thought I could buy you dinner," Esme suggested. "You know, get away from this, get something to eat, collapse into bed snoring like the old boring people we are."

Tanya's foul temper dissolved into an amused snort. "Yeah, sounds about right. Fine. Let me ditch these scrubs. I'll be right out."

And she was. Took about ten minutes but Esme waited quietly. No humming now. She sure as hell didn't want to attract the attention of the evening shift head nurse. That man was a complete and total bastard on a level with Kesha. He'd haul both of them in and scold them until Esme's ears were ringing.

When she returned, Tanya's hair was still stringy but she'd pulled it back into a messy bun and tamed the wispy bits around her ears with about six too many hair pins. Maybe Esme could coax her into a shared shower later. Tanya always did like it when Esme washed her hair for her.

"Come on," Tanya said, already striding to the big double doors that led from the human habitat out into the rest of the station. "I could eat a Saurid raw right now. What a damned day. Six of the newbs got in a big fight over who was going to have to take 'the worst' room. They ended up breaking four noses, dislocating one wrist and one of the poor stupid bastards was already dealing with disorientation sickness. He didn't stop vomiting until we knocked him out."

Or maybe not.

"Sucky day," Esme commented.

"You?" Tanya asked as if she'd only just realized that maybe Esme's day had been crap as well.

"Eh, got to watch Kesha picking Tikhonovich to pieces," Esme said. "More amusing than anything else. Tikhonovich spent the rest of the day in the comm center trying to get a good answer for all of this."

She waved a hand at the bare steel walls of the main hallway through the habitat. Meant everything. Tanya got that. Instead of replying, she rolled her eyes. It was what it was and nothing they could do would change it. Short of someone going mad and murdering people they were stuck with this mess.

Hell, they were probably stuck with it even if someone did go on a murder spree. Cheap bastards back on Earth.

They prowled out of the habitat, both pausing at the double doors to look and breathe and allow their minds to adjust to the strangeness around them. Tanya did it by staring out into the void at the center of the station. Esme did it by looking for the t'Saoir scurrying around, tentacles wiggling as they waddled like penguins on their four short stubby legs. They were everywhere, all over the station, so anytime the weirdness got to Esme she'd find a t'Saoir and just notice how adorably weird they were.

Seriously. Slap tentacles on a purple penguin and double its legs and you'd be close. Except for the stalk eyes. Never had gotten used to those. Though Esme still snickered when the t'Saoir group she'd been staring at all raised their eye stalks to stare back at her in perfect unison.

"Stop staring at them," Tanya huffed, apparently done with her own way of dealing with the weirdness. "Come on. I'm starving. We've got to find something really filling to eat."

"Last Day of Joy there were some t'Saoir who had this blue meat with a really bad deep fry coating," Esme suggested. "We could see if they have more meat, take it to the group with that incredible spice mixture."

"Oh, I tried that!" Tanya said. "Let's do that. It was so good."

When she smiled it lit the whole place up. Esme grinned and followed Tanya. No surprise, every single alien, t'Saoir included, got the hell out of their way. Humans on the hunt for food? Every race agreed that you got out of the way. There was a herd of Saurids up ahead, the sort with the big frills shaped like rainbows. They all flushed lemon yellow in alarm and hurriedly shuffled away as Tanya and Esme stalked past them.

Tanya made a face. "I hate that."

"What?" Esme asked. "The way everyone runs?"

"Mm-hmm." Tanya looked almost sick over it. Understandable. She was a nurse. Last thing she wanted was to scare people.

Esme grinned. "Hey, it makes sense. Humans are Space Orcs and Earth is Space Australia. Everybody runs from you when you're from a death planet."

Her grin turned into delighted laughter as Tanya stumbled to a stop, staring at Esme. Only took about five seconds of shocked blinking before Tanya started doing that gigglesnort thing she did when she was really amused. She punched Esme in the shoulder and then led the way onwards, giggle-snorting every time an alien scurried out of their way.

Turned out that the t'Saoir with the blue meat and the ones with the awesome spice mix had teamed up. They had complete plates available for humans to eat with deep fat fried everything. Meat, veggies already known to be liked by humans and those damned seaweed slices. Which really were way too tasty.

Made Tanya giggle-snort some more as she watched Esme go back for a second serving of the seaweed slices. She was going to be teased for the rest of her life over it but damn it, those things were good. Terrible any way other than deep fat fried but like this? Nirvana.

They both bought some bits of dried meat to sneak back into their quarters. Esme added a basket of melon-berry fruit, something like strawberries but with a ripe melon taste to it. Which she nibbled on as they slowly ambled back towards the human habitat.

"You do that specifically to calm people down," Tanya said as they passed the lighted fountain and headed along the edge of the platform, despite its lack of a railing that would keep anyone from falling into the central open are of the station.

Too big, that whole thing. The station was hollow, built around a central core that hovered in the center doing who knew what. Esme had poked around, trying to find out. Pretty much everyone had tried, at least briefly, all the aliens and pretty much all the humans, too. Yannick had a long-term project of figuring the thing out but the 'Creators', mysterious flying aliens that apparently were immortal and all-knowing who refused to leave their core, had made the computer system of the station unbreakable.

Or unbreakable by human means.

Didn't stop Yannick from trying. Looking out over the hundreds of miles-wide void at the center of the station, Esme couldn't blame him. She'd love to know who the Creators were. And damn if she wouldn't like to know how the hell they kept this cobbled together mess of a station together.

Tanya poked her.

"Sorry," Esme said with a wave for the void. "Distracted. Yeah, I do. If a human's got food in their hand they're not hunting. They're not a threat. Calms everyone down. It's part of why Kesha's as fat as he is. He never sets foot outside without something to eat in his hands. Tikhonovich is going to have to be careful. He's got that lean hunter look about him. Aliens are going to scatter from him whenever he approaches."

Tanya stopped in her tracks, staring at Esme. She looked around, eyes wide, and then pointed a finger at Esme while making vague little horrified noises. Esme grinned.

"Yup, you're a lean, mean hunter, love," Esme said. "I'm a lazy grazer, not a threat at all."

"You could snap my spine and drop me over the side so fast no one noticed that it happened," Tanya hissed at her. Low enough that no one heard her. "I'm made of marshmallows, Esme. No muscle tone at all."

"Now, that's nonsense," Esme replied. She popped one of the fruits into Tanya's mouth, prompting her to roll her eyes and snatch a handful from Esme's little basket. "You heft patients around all day long. You've got muscle. Just no training in hurting people."

"My point."

They both went still as a flock of Nikiphoros flashed past them, squeaking with alarm calls. They were followed by a pack of running t'Saoir whose eye stalks were extended a good foot and a half over their stocky little bodies. Kind of surprising how fast they could move when they really wanted to. They did a sort of galloping thing where they leaped forward, bounding like a gazelle, just on short stubby little legs.

Then they ducked as a cluster flailing Dancers, three Icalgra with their ice-blue scales pushed out like a porcupine who'd been attacked, one very alarmed Egraq all surged past them. Other than the Egraq who slithered towards them, jerked to a stop and then slithered past only when it saw that they both had food in their hands.

"Huh, it really does work," Tanya commented as she ate another melon-berry. "What's setting them off?"

"Either a pack of the fur babies on the hunt or our new commander," Esme said, offering Tanya a coin.

"Don't call them fur babies," Tanya huffed as she pulled a coin of her own. "That's terribly rude. And it's more likely to be the Creators flying by."

Esme snorted and then grinned as a pack of Withco, the aforementioned fur babies, dashed by. Cutest damned aliens on the whole station. They looked like Maine Coones about a thousand pounds bigger and with stingers on their tails. Purred like a literal jet engine if you could get close enough to scratch behind their ears. And were generally done with touching just as abruptly as any cat would be.

Behind the fur babies was Kesha, doing that rolling stroll thing of his where he looked slow and sleepy as any Saurid, with Tikhonovich by his side doing the 'holy fuck, what the hell have I gotten myself into' face that every newb got when they stepped out into the station.

"Esme," Kesha called, smiling at her as he rolled their way. "What you got there?"

"Fruit," Esme said. She offered it to Tikhonovich with a stern nod that actually got him to take it. "Try 'em. They're good. And if you have food in your hands the aliens won't panic seeing you."

"Ah... thank you." Tikhonovich took one, put it in his mouth and chewed but he clearly tasted it just as much as if he'd been eating sawdust.

"Pay up," Esme said, snapping her fingers both to Tanya who stuck her tongue out at Esme and at Tikhonovich.

Took the coin from Tanya. Had to snap her fingers again at Tikhonovich while Kesha snickered and rubbed his belly.

"For... what precisely?" Tikhonovich asked. He didn't reach for his pocket.

"We all pay for our own food," Esme said. "I bought those. Don't mind spotting you this time but I put my own pay into it. I expect to be compensated for it. Or you can give it back and deal with the terror you cause, you alpha predator in a human suit, you."

Predictably, Tanya burst into giggle-snorts, turning away so that she wasn't laughing straight into Tikhonovich's face. Kesha didn't bother at all. He just bellowed a laugh, slapping Tikhonovich in the back so hard he damn near knocked the man over. Seriously, how could anyone believe that Kesha was harmless. Paunch or not, the man was built like a tank and twice as powerful as one.

Tikhonovich glowered at Kesha but he dug into his pocket and pulled out a bunch of change. Esme looked, picked out three coins that marked a fair value for that amount of fruit with a recyclable basket and nodded.

"That's about what it's worth," Esme said and grinned at the suddenly sharp look in Tikhonovich's eyes. "Basket's recyclable. Make sure you have Kesha show you where to redeem it. Make some of your money back that way. We'll be going. Have a good stroll. Make sure you eat something while you're out. Sirs."

She nodded to them, then pushed Tanya away, back towards the habitat. Not a good thing that Kesha and Tikhonovich were out without escorts. Kesha pretty much never did that. He always made sure to bring a few people with him when he wandered about. Both to record what happened and have people to carry stuff for him. Hated carrying things, Kesha did.

But he probably wanted a nice quiet discussion with Tikhonovich well away from listening human ears. And the bugs that everyone knew filled the habitat. Couldn't blame him. Someone had to bring Tikhonovich up on how things worked on the Final Oblivion. Esme was just glad it wasn't her.

"So, you think you got energy for some private time?" Esme asked only to laugh as Tanya glared at her so scornfully she could have left scorch marks on armor plating.

"Don't be ridiculous," Tanya said. "I have a double shift tomorrow. Plus those newbs want to do an audit of all our systems. Something about getting us upgrades to the equipment."

Esme rolled her eyes just as Tanya did. Yeah, Kesha really

needed to fill Tikhonovich in on things around here. Upgrades. Yeah. Right. That'd be the day.

DAY HUNT on the Final Oblvion is now available at all major retailers in ebook and TPB format.

OTHER BOOKS BY MEYARI MCFARLAND:

AFTERWORD

This collection has some of my favorite shorts I've written in a long, long time. I can't say why. I just like them. They pull at my heart and make me happy when I read them.

Building families is probably my all-time top trope. Blood family is good, of course. I loved my parents and they were pretty darn good, overall. My brother's a great guy and he's living a good life with his wife and kids.

Found family, chosen family, though, that's where my heart is and will always be. So yeah, this collection makes me smile.

If you want more stories like this, please go sign up for my newsletter on www.MDR-Publishing.com. You'll get updates on whatever I've got coming up, special deals and you can get a free ebook or collection of my short stories. Or you can sign up at my Patreon and get news of any new stuff I publish plus awesome rewards.

Thank you for reading!

Meyari McFarland

March, 2024
www.MDR-Publishing.com

AUTHOR BIO

Meyari McFarland has been telling stories since she was a small child. Her stories range from SF and Fantasy adventures to Romances, but they always feature strong characters who do what they think is right no matter what gets in their way.

Her series range from Space Opera Romance in the Drath series, to Epic Fantasy in the Mages of Tindiere world. Other series include Matriarchies of Muirin, the Clockwork Rift Steampunk mysteries, and the Tales of Unification urban fantasy stories, plus many more.

You can find all of her work on MDR Publishing's website.

MORE FROM MEYARI MCFARLAND

Website:
www.MDR-Publishing.com

SOCIAL MEDIA:

Patreon - https://www.patreon.com/meyarimcfarland
    Mastodon – https://wandering.shop/@MeyariMcFarland
    Pillowfort - https://www.pillowfort.social/Meyari
    Facebook   -   https://www.facebook.com/meyari.
mcfarland.5
    Pinterest - https://www.pinterest.com/meyarim/

If you enjoyed this story, please leave a comment on your favorite site. Also, please sign up for the newsletter so that you can hear about the latest preorders and new releases.

Milton Keynes UK
Ingram Content Group UK Ltd.
UKHW041903120324
439302UK00005B/267

9 781643 091273